I0724254

Enlighten Me

Enlighten Me:
A Young Adult Novella and Bible Study

Bree Ann Fortney

To

Bear and Weasel

A Preface

There are more than thirty parables in the Bible—stories told by Jesus to illustrate spiritual lessons. But the meanings of these stories, referred to by God as "riddles" in the book of Ezekiel, are not intended to be easily discernable. It might sound a little strange, but Jesus doesn't use parables, containing common situations, to make things easy to understand. On the contrary, he uses them, in part, to create confusion. Jesus explains in the book of Matthew that his teachings reveal truth only to those who want to know it. What he is saying, in other words, is that those committed to the Kingdom of God will seek further understanding, while those who are not committed will reject the stories as nonsense.

Putting intentions aside, Jesus' parables *do* contain people, places, and situations relatable to everyday life—that is, everyday life over two thousand years ago. With mention of slaves and masters, long-forgotten illnesses, and ancient tribes, these teachings could be deemed even harder to decipher today than they were in Jesus' time. It is my hope that the following story—a modern-day interpretation of twelve of Jesus' parables—will help readers better understand these teachings and how they relate to their own lives.

The Study Guide section at the end of the book includes all of the referenced parables, the corresponding chapters of the story, and a brief commentary on their meanings. They are followed by questions for further exploration of how the parable is represented in the story, as well as for self-reflection.

In an effort to preserve the integrity of Jesus' parables, the messages in this book are intentionally subtle and, like the parables themselves, require deeper examination—by all those who are committed to the Kingdom of God!

OBITUARY

Sugar Hollow Daily News
Anna Felicity Hughes
In Loving Memory

Anna Hughes, aged forty-two, passed away June 2, 2019, at Sugar Hollow Memorial Hospital. Born March 2, 1977, in Newport News, Virginia, Anna was a proud Virginia resident her entire life.

Anna was a beloved piano teacher in Sugar Hollow. When not teaching, Anna enjoyed baking for our local delicatessen, "Dad's Deli," owned by her surviving husband, Keith Hughes. Anna is also survived by her twin sons, Oliver and Julian Hughes.

Anna's tragic death was caused by sepsis, a serious infection that can affect major organs in the body. The family asks that, in lieu of flowers, donations could be made to the Sepsis Foundation.

1
Julian

September, three years later

"Is *that* what you're having for breakfast?" my father asked in his stereotypical parent-voice. His tone told me this wasn't a question at all, but a judgment on my nutritional choices. A frosted chocolate donut filled my mouth, precluding an immediate answer.

"Morning," Oliver mumbled as he staggered sleepily into the kitchen, interrupting my donut standoff with Dad. *Ah! Saved by the twin brother*. Ollie was dressed for school, but clearly not yet awake. He headed to the counter and frowned, looking crestfallen at the empty box of donuts. Then, he looked back at me with a confused expression. Or maybe it was betrayal; I wasn't quite sure.

"Julian," my dad continued, his bushy brown eyebrows scrunched together, "you can't just eat donuts for breakfast."

"Then why did we buy them?" I righteously asked.

Dad let out a small sigh of defeat and shook his head (because he knew good and well that he *was a major contributor* to finishing off that box of a dozen donuts).

He capitulated with a small groan. "At least have a bowl of cereal to go with it. A donut is not enough for breakfast."

At that moment, Harry, our Border Terrier, started howling at the front door (indicating he had passed the "scratching at the door" stage, clearly having been ignored). His pathetic whine served as a sufficient distraction, allowing me to get up from the table without getting cereal.

"Ollie, can you work after school today?" My dad turned to my brother suddenly. "I need to get some office work done." My dad owned the town's delicatessen, appropriately named "Dad's Deli," here in good ol' Sugar Hollow, Virginia. It was actually started by my grandfather over fifty years ago. Right now, it could be described as vintage, with its vinyl-covered booths, black and white tiled floor, and retro signs, but the truth is, it wasn't retro intentionally; it just hadn't been remodeled since Grandpa built it.

"Can't," Ollie answered, glaring at me as I licked the frosting from my fingers. "I have baseball practice." *Ah yes! Baseball.* Ollie is a star player on the Varsity Baseball team, even though he was only a freshman last season. My twin and I are actually not much alike. He's tall and lean, with short, light brown hair. I'm more like my dad, with thick, dark brown hair and a broad build—but we both have the same green eyes, like my mom. Ollie is the athlete and the scholar. I'm the delinquent.

Harry started howling louder and jumping against the door, as if he could push it open with his front paws.

"It's September. Nice try. Your season doesn't start until, what? February?" Dad continued.

"January. Officially. But the coach thought it was a good idea for returning players to go to the batting cages together, once a week," Ollie mumbled while pulling out a box of pop tarts. Harry moved over to my dad, sitting at his feet and looking up at him with a forlorn look similar to Ollie's when he'd spied the empty box of donuts.

"Julian, go walk the dog," my dad snapped in irritation, standing up to put his dishes in the dishwasher.

"I can work after school," I volunteered with a shrug. Not like I had anything better to do.

"Really? Thanks Julian." My dad eyed me suspiciously. Even though I worked my fair share at the deli, it wasn't a secret to anyone that I didn't enjoy it and often came up with elaborate excuses as to why I couldn't work. "I appreciate you stepping up; thanks," Dad nodded in approval.

I answered with a smile and slight nod of my own before grabbing Harry's leash.

#

Normally, I wait for Ollie before walking to school, but today I wanted to meet up with my friend Felix. I found him immediately in his normal hangout, behind the baseball bleachers. He was sitting on the ground next to Ben, quickly scribbling something in a notebook—probably a copy of Ben's algebra homework.

"What are you doing?" I asked while approaching.

"What does it look like I'm doing?" he answered, without bothering to look up.

"Copying homework you could have done yourself in about ten minutes yesterday—when the teacher gave us time to do it in class?"

Felix just smirked in return.

"I need a favor," I continued.

"Speak."

"Can I go to your dad's garage Saturday and borrow his welder? I'm working on my mom's exhaust."

"Ah, the *Dodge*!" Felix replied with more affection in his voice than when he spoke of his own mother. *Yes, the Dodge*. Technically, it belonged to my dad now, but he agreed I could use it when I got my license if I fixed it up. It was a 1970 Dodge Charger with its original dark metallic green paint. It belonged to my mom before she died, and she had cherished the car for as long as I could remember. I'd already fixed the vinyl roof and replaced some gauges. But now I needed to tackle some bigger problems.

"The shop is too busy on Saturday. How about Sunday night? Around six? I can meet you there and give you a hand," Felix offered.

"That would be awesome, thanks. And thank your dad for me too." The bell rang, just as Felix finished his homework and slipped his books away.

#

School was a mind-numbing blur of boredom and monotony, as usual. That is, until I got pulled out of Spanish class, the last period of the day. We were practicing a conversation about going to the library when the phone rang.

"Hola?" Ms. Torres answered, her eyes immediately seeking me out.

What did I do this time? I wondered, racking my brain for all my recent misdemeanors. I was told to go to the Guidance Office, so I guess I was about to find out.

I walked down the empty hall of lockers and down the corridor toward Mrs. Patel's office. I knocked on the open door and she gestured toward the chair in front of her desk.

"Julian. You were late for school. Again. And you seem to have missed P.E. class . . . again," she said as her way of greeting. She placed her index finger on the bridge of her nose, pushing up her red-rimmed glasses.

"Um, shouldn't I go to the Principal's Office, then?" I asked, confused. Her eyes widened in response. I quickly amended, "Not that I'm complaining about avoiding detention. I was just curious as to why I'm here." Mrs. Patel tilted her head and gave me a sad smile, one I've seen many times before on others. It was a look of pity.

"What's going on with you, Julian?" she began, leveling her gaze at me. "You are smart and popular. I hear you're a star in your mechanics class. Why do you treat school like some kind of inconvenience? Like it's of no consequence? Because let me tell you, Julian—there are consequences."

I remained quiet for an uncomfortable minute before Mrs. Patel filled the silence. "I tried reaching out to your dad, but I don't think he actually *heard* me."

Oh, he heard her, all right. He heard that she thought I needed a professional to talk to after my mother died of sepsis three years ago. My dad does *not* believe in therapy.

"Tell me, Julian," she coaxed. "How can I help you? I

want you to like school. I want you to do well." *And she wants me to graduate so she can get me out of her hair,* I thought, but wisely kept quiet.

"How about if we try getting to know each other better. Then you might trust *me* to help? Let me think. How about I'll tell you something that . . ." she drew out the sentence and scanned the room for inspiration. Her eyes landed on a picture on her desk, then she continued, " . . . something that made me laugh recently. Then *you* go, ok?"

I nodded, but only because I didn't think I had a choice. I half-listened to her story about her cat chasing a ladybug, then landing inside a trashcan. All I could think about was her plump, Persian cat, probably resembling Mrs. Patel, herself, with grey-ish white hair and a well-fed appearance. When she was finished, she folded her hands neatly on her desk and gave me a pointed look. It was my turn to share something that made me laugh. I told her the first thing that came to mind.

"My dog suffers from pareidolia. Bet you don't know what that is, do you?"

"No," she chuckled, as if it were a rare thing to stump her, "can't say that I do."

"It's the tendency to see faces in inanimate objects. Ollie and I self-diagnosed our dog, Harry, when we were seven years old. It happened one night when my parents were watching some game show—Jeopardy, I think it was. The host gave the answer, and the contestants had to guess the question.

"So the host said in his announcer voice, '*This* is the tendency to perceive patterns or images, especially faces, in random shapes and lines, as in one famous example: The Face on Mars.' When a contestant answered, he pronounced the word wrong. He pronounced the 'do' part of the word like 'doo' instead of 'dough.' Ollie tried to hold in a laugh, which slipped out anyway with this weird squeak. And you know how, the harder someone tries to hold in a laugh, the more impossible it is? Once my parents shushed us for the third time, my mom tried a different tactic. 'Oliver, do you understand what the word means?' she asked my brother, while I was laughing so hard it hurt. Ollie was the smart one. He got it right away without my mom having to dumb it down. 'Yeah, he just said it. It's seeing faces on things that aren't really there. Like seeing shapes in the clouds,' he explained.

"'That's correct!' My mom shouted a little too loud. Even as a kid, I could see Ollie was the smart one." I shrugged.

At this, Mrs. Patel's smile faltered a bit, replaced with one that didn't quite reach her eyes.

"Then I got my own genius idea," I continued. "I started shouting, 'Uh, oh! Like Harry! Like when he barks at the neighbors' trash bags filled with leaves!'

"Now Ollie was laughing again. Even my dad joined in, nodding his head in agreement that Harry needed 'professional help'."

I paused in remembrance, my smile more genuine than it had been in a while. But then it fell like a leaf from a September Maple. "That's one of the last memories I have when I can remember all of us laughing like that. Together."

There was silence when I finished. I don't think either one of us knew what to say. So, I decided it was best to just get up and leave. Which is what I did. School would be over in a matter of minutes, so I grabbed my bag, swung it over my shoulder and headed to the parking lot to hang out with Felix, blowing off work at the deli.

#

> J? Where r u? Dad said you're a no
> show for work, now I have 2 go.

Sorry, Ollie. Was running an
errand with Felix and lost track
of time . . . thx for covering.

> Why can't you go now? I'm practic-
> ing with the team.

I'm over an hour away. Really
sorry. Besides, Dad likes it
when you work anyway . . . Last
week I cleaned that place top to
bottom, did the inventory, and
got caught up on stocking. Did he
even say thank you? Nope.

> Dude—that's what we get paid to
> do. And not even the point.

Might not matter to you, but it
matters to me.

> Do you ever say thank you to Dad?
> Huh??

Seriously???

Sorry again. Gotta go. Thx.

2
Oliver

Emulation. It's the word-of-the-day on my desk calendar. I kinda hate it. The calendar, that is, not the word. Learning new words was my mom's thing. She used to say in a superior voice (not at all matching her personality) that words were "candy for the brain."

She kept a small leather notebook of words she'd heard or read somewhere but didn't know. Then she would look them up and try to use them in conversation, like they had always been part of her *vernacular* (another one of her favorite words, meaning "everyday language").

When Mom died, I couldn't just let her collection of words—or her passion for discovering them—die with her. So, I kept her notebook and got my stupid word-of-the day calendar. How could I not? Her word collection was as important to her as my dad's collection of old tin soldiers he'd had since he was a kid. Or even my collection of baseball cards. Or Julian's—well, Julian doesn't collect anything except problems. I was just trying to do the right thing, but now it was just a daily reminder that she was gone. So there I was, studying the word "emulation."

/ˌemyəˈlāSH(ə)n/

"ambition or endeavor to equal or excel others. But in biblical times, it meant 'envious rivalry.'"

I crumpled the daily calendar page into a ball and threw it in the trash like a basketball free throw, cheering out loud as I made the shot.

"The crowd goes wild!" Julian mocked me, appearing at my bedroom door. I smiled.

"What are you up to today?" he asked.

"Dad doesn't need me, so I'm going to do some stuff for my photography club."

Photography was another of my mom's old hobbies, but I actually didn't even know about it until she was gone. We were packing up some of her things for the attic when I came across an old film camera. My dad was excited to show me how to use it, and ever since then I kinda fell in love with it.

Julian perused my room, fingering papers, books, and junk I had lying around. I could tell he was bored.

"You could come with me," I suggested hopefully. We used to spend a lot of time together, but ever since we'd started high school, we'd been drifting, our interests and friends pulling us in different directions.

"Maybe," he answered hesitantly while picking up a stray baseball, repeatedly tossing it in the air and catching it.

"This week's assignment is candid shots. Here," I remembered suddenly, taking out some recently developed photos. I showed him a picture of Hannah, a woman who had been baking and working in the deli since Grandpa owned it. She had been a part of our family for years.

"Holy crap. I don't know how it's possible, but you made Hannah look even older than she is. Look at those wrinkles!" Julian teased. True, Hannah's face had more creases than my word-of-the-day castoff, but there was something beautiful in her expressive blue eyes. I snatched the photo from his hand and laid it back on my desk with irritation.

"I'm kidding! I'm kidding!" he quickly rebounded, arms up in mock surrender. "It's actually really good." Julian let his gaze rest upon the photo, slowly turning his smirk into a genuine smile. "Hannah will probably outlive us all," he added.

"No kidding."

"So, who are you taking pictures of today?"

"I don't know. I thought I'd just go for a walk around town—"

"—and take pictures of strangers without them knowing? That's not creepy, is it?" Julian asked, his voice dripping with sarcasm. I raised my eyebrows with a knowing smile.

"*That's* why I have a telephoto lens, *genius*."

#

An hour later, the two of us set out walking toward a small neighborhood within our community, less than a mile from our home. We lived in a development made up of mostly two-story houses standing less than ten feet apart from one another, with quiet cul-de-sacs and large pine trees. It was built over twenty years ago, so sidewalk cracks and potholes were as common as the crooked mailboxes with chipped paint at every other house we passed. Well-worn dirt paths crisscrossed the surrounding fields, making it easy to hike to the nearby mountains. But for now, Julian and I stuck to the familiar sidewalk along the streets we knew by heart.

New houses were slated to be built close by, so I thought maybe I could get pictures of the construction workers. Instead, other people captured my interest—a young boy carving a pumpkin with his mom on their front porch, an elderly man sitting in his rocking chair, engrossed in a newspaper, and a parked moving van with a nervous-looking girl standing sentry.

I couldn't see much with my naked eye, but with the 300mm telephoto lens I'd borrowed from school, I could see every last detail. The girl by the moving van looked about my age, with long, velvety brown hair that reminded me of the rich bark color of a Cherry tree. She kept twisting her wrist, fidgeting with some sort of bracelet. I could even see her biting her lip, her eyebrows gathering nervously while the moving men lugged her belongings in a robotic routine they'd probably performed hundreds of times before. The glassy, bored look in their eyes was a contrast to the girl's obvious unease. I can't say I blamed her; I guess I'd feel the same way if my whole world were being hastily shuffled around in boxes. The camera clicked readily, allowing me to capture each millisecond of this poor girl's torture.

"That clicking makes you sound like the paparazzi," Julian harassed me.

"As long as she doesn't hear it; I don't want to make an impression as a stalker," I explained while holding the camera up to my eye, trying to find the right angle.

"Make an impression? Wait . . . you mean you want to *meet* her? Give me that camera," Julian said, snatching the Canon out of my hands.

Too bad the strap was still around my neck, so he jerked me right along with it, our heads almost smacking into each other. He held the camera up to his eye, as I remained uncomfortably close.

"Oh, she's pretty, all right! In a 1950s kind of way. Is she really wearing a *poodle* skirt?"

"Shut up," I scolded, trying to grab the camera back, but failing. "It's just a normal skirt. I see plenty of girls wear them."

"*Oh*," Julian exclaimed with a new sarcastic tone. "I didn't know you had such an eye for fashion, what with that collection of plain cotton t-shirts you own."

"Whatever. Just give me back the camera." I pulled, but Julian had a few pounds of muscle on me and was not in a hurry to let go.

Something in his expression changed suddenly, making me nervous. He looked happy; *too* happy. "Maybe I'll take some pictures, too," he started, holding the camera to his eye while my head was practically resting on his shoulder. "Hey, pretty girl!" he shouted. "Smile!"

My face flushed as I elbowed him in the side and grabbed the camera back. He tried to regain control but I twisted out of reach. All the while he was convulsing with laughter and howling between breaths, *"Ollie has a girlfriend! Ollie has a girlfriend! Nya nya nya nya nya."*

"You jerk," I hissed, but he was laughing so hard now I had a hard time keeping from laughing myself. I grabbed his elbow to pull him away and flee the scene, but he dug his boots into the ground. It was like trying to pull a pit-bull off a squirrel. He finally gave way, landing on top of me, and making a scene for the entire population on the street to gawk at. At this, we both tried to collect ourselves between belly laughs, heaved ourselves up, and ran the entire way home.

3
Oliver

Two weeks later

"Alright class, pop quiz time. Get out a piece of paper and a pencil," Mr. Dubanowski announced with as much enthusiasm as a school bus driver on a Monday morning. The predictable cacophony of groans and grievances filled the classroom, along with the sounds of backpack zippers and sheets of paper being ripped from spiral notebooks. I was reaching for *my* notebook when I felt a pencil poke me in the back.

"What?" I mouthed silently to Julian. He answered by holding up a small, folded piece of paper. My eyes widened as I attempted to silently convey to my brother, *Not now, we're taking a quiz!*

Either my facial expression was not clear enough, or—more likely—Julian just didn't care. He insistently pushed the note at me.

I was pretty sure I could read what he was mouthing: *I don't care; just take the stupid note!*

I read it hesitantly, stealing glances at the teacher to make sure the note remained undetected. Mr. Dubanowski liked to make a production out of reading notes aloud to the class when he caught people passing them. Not to mention, our dear old (did I forget to mention "old"?), cantankerous math teacher liked to hand out detention slips like a Labrador Retriever liked giving wet kisses. The note read:

Isn't that the girl you were taking pictures of yesterday? Don't go straight home after school. Meet me by the baseball field bleachers. Need to talk to you and can't do it at home.

I didn't want to write back, but I was afraid my silence would imply consent. I quickly scribbled back before the rest of the class got settled for the quiz:

Can't. Have work after school. And yeah, that's her.

I threw the note over my shoulder while Mr. Dubanowski was reading out the quiz questions in his hands. I heard it hit Julian's desk right as the teacher looked up.

"Alright," Mr. Dubanowski began, "I will put five equations on the board. Solve them for 'A', showing your work, like the last quiz, and the one before that, get it? When you are done, put it on my desk and work on tonight's homework. Do not—I repeat—do not forget to put your name on the paper. Three of you flunked the last quiz for lack of a name. I am confident those three will remember, but there are twenty-three others, and as much as I recognize the difficulty some of you have writing your own name, I assure you the effort will be lavishly rewarded. I will not play 'guess who's handwriting this is' if you forget."

Mr. Dubanowski's sarcasm was the only defining feature to his otherwise dull personality. He turned to write on the board when I felt another pencil poke. Just when I had decided to ignore my brother, a note flew over my shoulder, landing in the middle of my desk. Panic rising, I quickly snatched it, almost as a reflex, hiding it in my fist. I opened the crumpled note, half-hidden by the desk:

It won't take long.

I didn't have time to respond. Mr. Dubanowski was done writing on the board, and I knew, from experience, within the next minute he would commence his somber walk up and down the aisles, surveying our work. I didn't want to get caught in the act of writing Julian back. Plus, I knew that when Julian wanted something, resistance was futile. I sighed deeply and audibly, loud enough for him to hear me—my only means of protest.

4

Darla

Four minutes earlier

"They're twins," the girl next to me said in a matter-of-fact tone, answering my unspoken question. I felt my face redden, as I knew she'd just caught me staring at them.

"Um, what?" I tried to play it off.

"Julian and Ollie. They're twins. The guys you're staring at?" she replied knowingly, as I silently prayed my blush didn't get any worse. I didn't think I was being *that* obvious. I futilely tried to deny it.

"Oh, uh, no. I wasn't—" I weakly began when she cut me off.

"It's ok. I get it. They're totally cute. Ollie is the one with the shorter hair in the black Henley. Julian's obviously the one with the darker, disheveled hair and grey hoodie. They have the same green eyes. Totally weird, right? I mean, I know they're twins, but their eyes are, like, so similar! I'm Harlow, by the way. You're new, right? That must be so hard to move in when the school year has already started. What's your name?"

"Darla," I interjected quickly. For some reason I felt compelled to talk as fast as Harlow was.

"Oh, cute! What a pretty name!" she replied.

I hated my name. When I was in second grade, my teacher started calling me, "Darling Darla," and praised me in front of the class for being such a "good little girl." The nickname stuck among the students as well, but not as a compliment. "Darling Darla can't play kickball. She might get dirt on her dress!" they'd tease. Or, "Don't tell Darling Darla a secret; she's such a *good girl* she'll tell the teacher." What made it worse was that I *was* a girly-girl—and I did try hard to do the right thing—so the name kind of fit. I liked wearing dresses, playing with dolls, and wearing pretty bows in my hair. But in fourth grade I tried to rebel against my darling "reputation" by giving a girl in school—one of the popular, cool girls—the answers to a test. I thought it would finally show everyone that I wasn't such a good girl after all, and maybe they'd even drop the nickname or call me something like "Daring Darla" instead. It didn't work, though. I hated the look of disappointment in the teacher's eyes when I admitted I'd helped a girl cheat. Plus, I got in so much trouble with my dad that I decided it was much easier just to be myself. So, I was back to being "Darling Darla" in a matter of days.

"What do you think of the school? Oh—" Harlow interrupted herself, "—who do you have for science? And why did you move here so late in the year?"

The problem with Harlow's rapid-fire interrogation was

that the answer to the last question couldn't really be abbreviated.

"My parents got divorced—" I started hesitantly, but then Harlow cut me off. *Again.*

"Oh yeah, I totally get it." She waved the topic off like a fly. "So, who do you have for science?"

Ok, so maybe it *was* as simple as that: my parents got divorced, and we moved. Happens all the time, right? At least I didn't have time to dwell on it, as the questions kept coming. I tried to answer as many as I could, like a contestant on a timed game show, when Harlow circled back to the first topic.

"So, which Hughes brother were you staring at? That's Julian and Ollie's last name, by the way," Harlow continued, casually tossing her dark wavy hair off her shoulder, her long bangs obscuring her eyes like a sheepdog.

"Well, I think I may have seen them—"

"Alright class," a voice droned, saving me from answering. At the front of the room I saw an older, stout-looking man (presumably the math teacher). "It's pop quiz time. Get out a piece of paper and a pencil."

5
Oliver

Later that day

After last period, I went to my locker to pick and choose what books to take home. Then, I headed straight to the baseball field, hoping I could help Julian with whatever he needed and head to the deli. Time seemed to be against me lately, as I was always cramming in extra hours at the deli to help pay my way into college, extra baseball practice to keep my batting average up, extra homework to keep my grades up . . . not to mention having to cover for Julian when he bailed, which seemed to be happening a lot lately.

As I rounded the corner from the school courtyard, I saw Julian sitting on the cold aluminum bleachers looking up at the clouds. "What's up?" I asked, hoping this wasn't about needing money. Last time I lent him money to buy new brake pads for Mom's Dodge, I never saw it again—the money, that is.

"I need to talk to Dad tonight, and I need you to back me up on something." He paused for a second.

"This can't be good."

"I want to move in with Aunt Sarah."

I flinched. I couldn't have been more shocked than if he'd told me he wanted to be a professional ballerina and wear a pink tutu. "You mean in California?" I finally asked.

"No, Aunt Sarah in Egypt! Unless you know another Aunt Sarah, then yep—California."

"Don't be sarcastic," I snapped. *How can he be making light of this?* I shook my head in total bewilderment. "Where's this coming from? We barely even talk to Aunt Sarah."

"I talked to her last week. She said I could stay in her guest room and finish my sophomore year there." He shrugged, as if he were simply telling me he was going to hang out at Felix's place after school.

"So, you've been planning this for a while? And you never told me?" I drummed my fingers on the bleachers, still struggling to process what my brother was saying. I couldn't deny I was really hurt. Although Julian and I weren't one to share our deep feelings, I'd always considered us to be pretty close—we were twins, for goodness' sake. Clearly I'd been mistaken all these years.

"Listen, Ollie. You know I love you man—"

"Nah ah," I stopped him, shaking my head vigorously. "No. Don't give me some cliché 'I love you' speech. Answer my question. Why?"

Julian straightened his back, his eyes distant. I could tell he was thinking about what to say next, trying to—I don't know—spare my feelings or win me over. But his clenched fists and the frown etched on his face spoke volumes.

"I hate it here," he said bitterly. "I'm not like you, ok? I don't like school, I don't get good grades, I don't have friends, and I hate working at the deli."

"You have friends—what about Felix?"

"We both know that Felix is an idiot; don't even pretend you like him. I have people I hang out with—but no real friends."

"Hang out with me and my friends," I suggested in a voice that sounded desperate, like a toddler begging his mom for some candy.

"So we can all hang out at the batting cages and talk about our top college choices and career objectives? No thanks. That's not me."

"What about me? What about Dad?" I countered, but Julian was done. The brief glimpse of honest emotion he showed me dried up like rain in the summer heat. All that was left was his resolve.

"Ollie, we'll always be close. Doesn't matter if I move away for a while. But stop making this about you, *please*," he pleaded. Looking at him then, and knowing how stubborn he could be, I knew I could never change his mind, even if I gave him a dozen reasons why I thought this was a bad idea.

"It's going to crush Dad," I warned.

"Hate to break it to you Ollie, but Dad's been crushed for a long time now. Me leaving? He'll probably be happy to see me go."

6
Oliver

The next week

I was putting the finishing touches on a pastrami on rye sandwich when I heard the chime of the bell above the door. I handed the finished product to the customer when I looked up and saw Darla, the new girl from my algebra class, standing next in line. She looked nearly as nervous as she did the day I'd watched her move into her new home.

"Hi. What can I get for you?" I asked, silently pleading to the gods above that she didn't see Julian and me outside her house a few weeks back.

"Hi, um . . . I wanted to get something for dinner," she said while perusing our sandwich board. "How about an Italian sub? With mayo, oil, and vinegar, please."

"Just the one?"

"Yup, just one," she answered with a slight look of confusion.

"What about your family?" I asked.

"Oh, no. It's just me. I mean, I do have a family. Well, I live with my mom and little brother. But they don't need dinner. I mean—they don't need me to get their dinner."

She stopped to collect her thoughts and smiled shyly. She was cute when she got flustered. I wondered if it was me making her nervous?

"I work two doors down at Pet Palace," she then explained, "and I'm working the late shift by myself, so I just thought I'd pick up a sandwich for dinner."

"Makes sense," I proclaimed, while unwrapping the salami. "You just moved here, right?" I asked, my back turned to her as I sliced the meat.

"Yeah, uh, I'm originally from North Carolina, but my mom wanted to relocate. I'm Darla, by the way."

"I know," I turned and answered with a smile, then went to get out the pepperoni from the meat case. "You're in my algebra class. And history, too, right?"

"Oh, yeah. That's right. So, you're Oliver?"

"Yup. But most people call me Ollie." I finished making the sandwich while the silence lingered, somewhat uncomfortably. I wasn't sure what to say, but I didn't want her to leave, either. I saw her twist and pull at her bracelet, like she did the day she moved in, so I thought that was a good place to start.

"What's that on your wrist?" I asked, not mentioning my observation that she liked to fidget with it.

"Oh this? It's a bracelet my mom gave me when I was baptized. It has a Bible verse on it that I like."

"Aren't people baptized as babies?" I asked. I knew awfully little about religion, except what I'd seen on TV and read in books. My parents had never really been the types to bring us to church.

"Some are," she explained with a slight shrug. Her brown eyes lit up when she spoke and she seemed to stand taller. "It depends on what religion you are and what you believe. I'm a Baptist, and Baptists typically get baptized when they are old enough to make a commitment for themselves."

"So, you believe in God and all that Jesus stuff?" *Jesus stuff?* I could hear how stupid that sounded before it even left my mouth and had to restrain myself from rolling my eyes at myself.

"Yes, I believe in God, and all that 'Jesus stuff,'" she said with cute smirk, like a parent would give a naïve child. "It's actually really important to me."

"I can tell." I nodded.

"Oh yeah? How?"

"It seemed so natural for you to talk about it. And," I continued, "you stopped fidgeting with your bracelet. So, what does the Bible verse say, anyway?"

"It says, 'I can do all this through Him who gives me strength.'"

"Cool." *Yep. That sounded intelligent.* I inwardly groaned. I wasn't really sure what else to say. It was cool that she believed in something—something that obviously gave her strength—but I wasn't really sure what the appropriate response was. I put her sandwich in a bag and rang her up, tossing in one of Hannah's famous pumpkin muffins for free.

I held the bag out to her, and she clasped the sides of the brown paper, but I was reluctant to let go. "What do you do when you're not in school and working at the Pet Palace?"

"I'm really into theatre. I used to take voice lessons and perform in the school plays back home." *Back home.* I wondered how long it took someone to feel at home after moving? I wondered if Julian would ever feel at home in California? My thoughts drifted for a minute before I realized that Darla was staring at me, I suppose because I hadn't let go of her bag. I released it and tried to cover for my awkwardness.

"Theatre, huh? We have a Spring Musical every year at school. It's a really big deal. There are even competitions with other high schools. Are you going to try out?"

Darla's smile widened. "I didn't know there was one. Right now I'm seriously just trying to remember where my classes are and catch up on all my homework. But, yeah, if I can swing it, I would totally try out for a school musical."

I saw Hannah glare pointedly at me over her shoulder as she mixed some fresh potato salad, a job I was supposed to do before my last break.

"Uh-oh. I gotta get back to work," I said, "but it was nice meeting you. I'll see you around school?" *Really, Ollie? That's the best you can do?*

"Yeah, sounds great. And thanks for the muffin," she added as she walked out the door and another customer walked in.

Hannah turned to me with the large mixing bowl in hand. "Since when do we give out free muffins?" she asked in a sing-song tone, her eyebrows raised knowingly.

"Mind your own business," I responded playfully, and as an afterthought, grabbed a dry dishcloth and lightly smacked her away.

7

Julian

The next day

Dinner wasn't usually a sit-down affair at our house, but we tried to have meals together at least a couple times a week. Dad insisted on it. Since we all did our fair share of cooking at the deli (whether it was baking pastries, making salads, or whipping up some hot sides), dinner was usually something quick and easy. Tonight? Hot dogs and baked beans, straight from can to microwave.

Ollie set the table in our small kitchen that had never felt quite the same since Mom died. The round oak table was adorned with a sage green paisley tablecloth. Like-colored ceramic canisters lined the counter, holding various serving utensils, and a sign that read, "But first, Coffee," sat above the refrigerator. All had been placed with careful consideration by Mom, and all were a touch too feminine for a house with just three guys.

There was something comical watching my dad—a Retired Air Force Sergeant and Gulf War veteran—eating beans off a plate decorated with a pink country rose pattern. But none of us would dare change anything. It was like an unspoken understanding: as long as we ate off Mom's plates and kept the décor she'd chosen, then a part of her was still there with us. Kind of.

We took our seats, and before we started eating, I decided I'd wasted enough time trying to find the "right time" to talk to dad about California. There was no point drawing it out any longer. So, I jumped right in. "Dad, I want to talk to you about something," I said, my voice wavering a little. "And I really need you to keep an open mind."

"I'm not giving you your mom's car, Julian," Dad said with a swift shake of his head. "You're too young and I'm not ready to give it up. We've been through all this."

"No, I know. It's not that." I couldn't believe how nervous I suddenly got. *It's now or never, I guess.* "I want to go live in California with Aunt Sarah." The words came out rapid-fire. I let out a deep breath and waited while my dad finished a bite of hot dog. Then, to my surprise, he leaned back in his seat and chuckled. *Has he heard me?* I wondered.

"Did anyone remember to feed Harry?" Dad asked.

"I'll do it," Ollie said suddenly, jumping from the table to fill the dog dish with kibble.

"Dad," I continued, "I'm being serious."

"What, you want to work on your tan and learn to surf?" he said dismissively, eating a forkful of beans. I could feel the back of my neck getting hot, and I rubbed it reflexively.

"No. I want to go somewhere that's *not here*," I blurted out. Now *that* caught my dad's attention. He put his fork back on his plate and looked me quizzically.

"You're serious? You mean you want to *move out*? You're fifteen years old—fifteen-year-olds don't move away from home." He gave an awkward laugh, but I could tell he was finally starting to let what I was saying sink in.

"Even if your aunt agreed to this, wouldn't you miss your friends, us . . .?" he said, his voice trailing.

"No," I lied, feeling defensive. "I don't have friends here. I hate working in the deli, and I'm tired of the same thing, day after day."

My dad now turned his attention to Ollie, who had very slowly made his way back to the table. He gave Ollie a *can you believe this?* look, to which Ollie just shrugged. *Coward.*

"What makes you think things would be any different in California?" he asked. Finally, Ollie cut in. "Dad, Julian is—" Well, he tried, before Dad interrupted him.

"Let him explain for himself, Oliver. You're not always going to be around to bail him out of trouble."

Ouch. That stung, even though I already knew my dad didn't think much of me.

"It can't be any worse than here. A fresh start, after everything we've been through, has to be a good idea," I persisted.

"What about Oliver?" Dad persisted. "He's your twin."

"Nooo, *really*?" I said with a little too much attitude for Sergeant Hughes' liking.

"Don't get fresh with me," he said, pointing his fork at me. An uneasy silence descended as the three of us shoveled in our beans and hotdogs. It felt like minutes before he spoke again. "Let's just eat our dinner," he said with the finality of a courtroom judge.

#

A week went by with almost complete radio silence in the house. Finally, my dad called me downstairs. In a very anticlimactic manner, he nodded his head at me and said, "I talked with your aunt. She agreed. You leave next week."

Then, he walked out of the room.

8
Charlotte

The next day

Today was a *good* day. I was killing it with my new Abercrombie & Fitch leather Moto jacket, my naturally curly red hair was behaving beautifully, Caleb Mitchel was rumored to want to ask me out, *and* I just got a B on an impossibly hard chemistry test. *Ah, it is so good to be me!*

I sauntered over to my usual lunch table, past the band geeks and book nerds, ready to share my news with my friends at the official "popular" table. Ada, Jill, Reagan, and Shauna were already seated when I made my approach. Before I could speak, Ada started crooning over me.

"Charlotte! Is that new? I *love* your jacket! Is it real leather?" Ada asked with an outstretched hand as if she were going to stroke it.

"Ew!" I pushed her hand away. "I'm not a *dog*, Ada. No

need to pet me." Snickers made their way around the table.

"Of *course*, it's real," I replied with a shrug.

"Did your dad buy it for you on a business trip?" Jill asked with only mild curiosity, as she gathered her thick blond hair into a messy bun. Getting new clothes wasn't exactly a rare occurrence for me. "Yes. And that's not all," I practically giggled. "I got the cutest midi skirt and boots to go with it."

"So unfair," Ada whined, lazily pushing pieces of salad around her bowl. "My dad would have no idea what to buy me at a clothing store."

At this, I heard an ugly snort from Jill, who had the nerve to chime in, "It's not like he picks them out *himself*, Ada. He obviously has a secretary or someone do it for him." She took a big bite of her sandwich. *Ouch! Jealous much, Jill?* I hoped my sudden cold stare in her direction made her rethink that line of conversation, and if her downcast eyes and sullen expression were any indication, it did.

"Anyway, moving on from my wardrobe, as fascinating as it is"—I rolled my eyes—"I have other news to share. I got one of the highest grades on Mrs. Hoffman's chemistry test," I said with smug satisfaction. Then, I unpacked my lunch while I let the news sink in. After all, I had a reputation to maintain as the most popular girl in my grade. Sure, I was pretty, the star of every school musical production, and everybody liked me, but I also had been on the honor roll every semester, and I intended to keep it that way.

At that moment, another one of our friends, Kennedy, bounced over, pulling a seat up from the empty lunch table next to ours and squeezing herself between Jill and Reagan. She was excited to share something with us, too, apparently, as she kept pushing her short, wavy hair behind her ears, struggling (and failing) to remain still. She painstakingly opened up her lunch cooler, pathetically trying to build up some suspense and keep the spotlight on her. *Amateur*.

"Guess what I got today?" she said in a sing-song voice, playing coy.

"A new acne cream?" I mumbled, earning a sideways glance and smirk from Jill.

"I got a B+ on Mrs. Hoffman's chemistry exam! Can you believe it?" she screeched like a howler monkey.

This was a big deal for Kennedy. Squeals of congratulations rang around our lunch table. Kennedy may be an awesome forward on the girls' soccer team, but her grade point average was embarrassingly low, however you measured it. Currently failing chemistry, Kennedy needed a good grade on this test to stay on the soccer team. When I didn't respond to her news right away like the others, Kennedy singled me out. Not to sound conceited, but my opinion mattered more than most. It just comes with maintaining one's status of being "most popular."

"Charlotte, can you believe it! I mean, it was a miracle I passed." She sighed heavily, trying to be humble. "I know you studied really hard for this test too, right? I bet you got, like, 100 percent, right?" she rambled.

I had a few choices here. Kennedy was my friend, sure, but there was no way I was going to tell her, and everyone else at the table, that I only got a B on that test. So, I could either:

A) Change the subject, suggesting we concentrate on her success and not mine or

B) Lie and tell her I got an A as usual.

After careful consideration, I went with option . . . C.

"Kennedy, you have a big piece of salad stuck in the middle of your front teeth. Gosh, have some self-respect and chew with your mouth closed." This earned some laughter at the table, momentarily changing the topic.

"Who's that new girl siting with Harlow?" Reagan interrupted. We all turned abruptly to look at a pretty girl with long brown hair—hair to *die* for.

"Oh, that's Darla. She just moved here," Ada explained.

"Obviously," I muttered.

"She's in my chorus class. She has the most amazing voi—" Ada stopped mid-sentence, eyes wide with fear. I knew what she was going to say.

So. Ada thinks you can sing, new girl? I wasn't worried. Even if she could sing better than I could, which was doubtful, I wasn't one for "healthy competition" when there were more guaranteed ways to success. I'd lived long enough to learn a valuable lesson: *There are two ways to win in life—you can win by running the swifter race, or you can make sure the competition is running more slowly.*

9
Hannah

November

As I watched Oliver float around the deli, robotically turning merchandise on the shelves so that all the labels neatly faced the same direction, I couldn't help but think about when I was his age. It felt like a lifetime ago, and I guess in a way it was. I worked, just as he did, at this very same deli, for his grandfather, Donald Hughes. I watched as Donald's son, Keith, took over. I grew to love Keith as if he were my own son. My husband Peter and I had never been blessed with children.

I remembered when Keith left for the war and came back a changed man. He hadn't known what he wanted from life when he got back from Iraq, but he started at the deli as a means to make money and move on. He never complained about the hard work, and I respected him for that. Perhaps what I deemed to be difficult was actually a reprieve from the experiences he'd had on his deployment. Although he never spoke about what he saw and what he did on his deployment, I could see the invisible scars.

He took to the business quickly, and I watched as he started to form a bond, not only with the customers, but with the deli itself. He clearly enjoyed what he did. I'm not sure at what point the job became a career, but it was obvious to me that he would happily follow in his father's footsteps and continue running this town jewel.

But not our Oliver. No; he was different from his father, with different aspirations.

I watched him as he hung up some of his photography work in the back of the shop. His father beamed with pride at the idea, not just because of his son's clear talent, but also because those pictures really brightened up the place. Gave it character. There were close-ups of the food we serve, a hauntingly beautiful picture of the empty booths at closing time, and a candid shot of his father laughing with a customer. They were impressive. God blessed him in many ways, and I just knew He had a plan for the boy.

"Hannah, what do you think of this one?" that girl from the pet shop called out, holding up a close-up picture of me mixing some cake batter.

She's not fooling anyone, always stopping by "just for lunch." She's smitten with Ollie. "Humph," I groaned. *Too many wrinkles in that photo.* The pet-shop girl handed the frame to Ollie, who was standing on a stepladder to position the photographs on the wall.

"Thanks, Darla." He smiled. Then she smiled. Neither seemed to know what else to do. *Ah, to be young again.*

"Hun, your sandwich is ready. I put a muffin in there, too, for you." I winked at her. *She's a sweet girl. Good head on her shoulders, too, if she likes our Ollie.*

"Thank you, Hannah! When are you going to tell me the secret ingredient to your muffins?"

"Honey, *I* am the secret ingredient." *Kids.*

10
Julian

The same day

California was exactly what I expected, and yet, not. The weather was consistently sunny, there was never a shortage of people outdoors—walking, running, rollerblading—and the beaches were crowded with surfers, even in November.

What I didn't expect was to be so lonely. Aunt Sarah explained that the area she lived in was transient; everyone was from somewhere else, and someone was always moving on. So, I was nothing special here. Just the opposite—I was someone to avoid because I would probably pick up and move someday, too.

One would think with my new high school having over 3,000 students, making friends wouldn't be such a challenge. But everyone seemed to already have their own groups and cliques, making it hard to join in. Finding a gastro pub, vegan avocado smoothie, or a fried oyster burrito? Easy. Making friends? Not so much.

At home, I'd had Felix, but we weren't all that close any-way. He was just someone I could play basketball with; someone who'd cut class with me and help me work on my mom's car. A guy who didn't care how well I did on an algebra test and who wouldn't ask about my future. I had Ollie to take care of all the big questions, but he had his own friends.

I took a bus my first few days, but on Friday, Aunt Sarah wanted to drive me to school. She pulled up in front, behind a long row of cars, driving her beyond awesome Chevy Corvette ZR-1. The love of cool cars must run in the family. Looking out the passenger window, I saw the school's massive bell tower and several courtyards, making the place look even bigger than a lot of college campuses back in Virginia.

After a brief good-bye, I grabbed my book bag and head-ed toward the front entrance. Before I could make it in, two guys with backpacks slung over their shoulders—one tall and skinny, with low-riding plaid shorts, the other more stocky-looking with a backward baseball cap—approached me.

"*That* is an awesome car," the taller of the two guys declared. "Your mom's?" he asked while watching my aunt pull out of the parking lot.

"Legal guardian," I said. The guy shot me a strange look—curiosity? I don't know why I didn't just say it was my aunt's.

"What year is it, '90?"

"Wow, yeah," I replied. "Impressive."

"You know about cars?" he asked with a disbelieving smile.

"Enough to know it has the only overhead-cam engine

in Corvette history." I got a nod of approval from the tall guy, while Baseball Cap just laughed at his friend mockingly, as if I'd somehow got one over on him.

"I'm Liam," Tall Guy said.

"Pete," Baseball Cap uttered, giving me a "nice-to-meet-you" nod.

"I'm Julian."

"New here?" Liam asked.

"Yeah, just started this week." At this point we were back to walking toward the school entrance, the first bell set to ring in a minute or two.

"Let me see your schedule," Liam asked. I reached behind me to unzip the lower section of my book bag and grabbed the slightly wrinkled piece of paper.

"You have to go to homeroom. If not, you are marked absent for the day. And you have to go to your fifth period history class. Mr. Albertson always checks the master attendance list to make sure no one cuts his class. The rest of them?" He shrugged. "Just make an appearance once in a while, then show up for mid-terms and final exams."

"Huh? You don't go to all your classes?" I asked.

"Nah," Liam answered, as if I had asked him if he would like a Pepsi.

"How do you manage to pass a year of high school if you're never there?" I pressed.

"Teachers don't care if we don't show up. They just care if we pass the tests. If we pass"—he held his fingers to his mouth and made a kissing gesture—"then we graduate. Trust me, they do not want us to be around for another year."

"But how do you pass final exams?"

"Ah. That *is* the question."

And apparently it was going to go unanswered, as he simply nodded his head again as if everything made sense now.

"Where do you go during school?" I continued my line of questioning.

"Meet me by the bell tower after first period—I have Mrs. Boesky; another one that checks attendance. I'll show you where we go."

I'd been down this road before, and I wasn't sure if I wanted to do it again. Wasn't the whole point of coming here to get a fresh start? Then again, this place was huge and it would be nice to make friends. What would it hurt to miss a few classes?

"Ok. See you then."

#

mailto: jwhughes@nethost.com
from: ollie.h78@nethost.com

hey j. how's CA? sick of all that sunshine yet? We got snow last week, but not enough to cancel school. Dad hired someone else for the deli. You may know the guy. He graduated two years before us. Hudson Baxley? He seems ok, I guess. He almost cut his finger on the deli slicer, so that was exciting. Talk about your red meat, ha! Oh, and I've been hanging out with Darla some. Hannah calls her "that pet-shop girl." Dad says hi. Gotta go work on a science project. Later.

mailto: ollie.h78@nethost.com
from: jwhughes@nethost.com

hey bro! California is awesome. Aunt Sarah says hi. Yeah, I think I remember Hudson. Skinny blond dude, right? Darla, huh? Are you dating? Poor girl must be heartbroken that the good-looking twin moved away. I met some guys at school that are pretty awesome, so things are good. Tell Dad I said hi. Gotta run.

mailto: jwhughes@nethost.com
from: ollie.h78@nethost.com

What are your new friends like? How is school? Is it really different from here?

mailto: jwhughes@nethost.com
from: ollie.h78@nethost.com

J—where have you been? It's been over a week since I've heard from you. Every time I try to call Aunt Sarah she says you're out with your friends, "living your best life," whatever that means. Has she always been so weird? Write me back.

11
Oliver

A few days later

What the cafeteria at Sugar Hollow High lacked in size, it made up for with the ear-piercing chatter of the masses. About fifteen round tables, accommodating over one hundred students, were spread out in the colorless room, motivational posters about "school spirit" lining the white, concrete walls.

I typically sat with my friends, who were also the guys on the baseball team, while Darla sat a few tables away with Harlow and some other girls I've seen her hang out with. After waiting in line for my unidentifiable mystery-meat and over-cooked vegetables, I set my tray down at my table and made my way over to her spot.

"Nice t-shirt." Harlow nodded in my direction as I approached. I looked down to remember what I was wearing—a white Pearl Jam t-shirt (I think it belonged to my dad), with my unzipped navy fleece jacket. I smiled and nodded my thanks and turned my attention to Darla.

"Gotta second?"

"Yeah, sure. What's up?" she answered, looking up at me from her seat. She wore her hair in a way I haven't seen before, some sort of intricate braid. It was pretty. Today she was wearing a light blue sweater dress with a belt tied around her waist, also pretty.

"Can we go outside?" I asked. Darla nodded in agreement, put down her water bottle, and followed me to the hallway. As soon as we made it far enough down the hall that the noise became less ear-splitting, we stopped and faced each other.

"I have it on good authority that the musical for this year has been chosen," I started.

"Really? What is it? How'd you find out already?" she asked in rapid succession, her brown eyes looking even brighter than normal.

"So, it's tradition for the seniors to vote on the production, and my friend, Brian, well, he's on the baseball team—he always works backstage. And he met with the theater teacher to see if baseball practice would interfere with stagehand meetings." I drew out my explanation. Darla waved me on to talk faster. "So, my friend—he's only a junior, and he wasn't supposed to be at the meeting, but he overheard . . ."

Darla stood on her tiptoes to look me in the eyes (although still not quite reaching) and gripped the sides of my fleece. "Are you trying to kill me slowly? What is it?" she shrieked. I just smiled. Slowly. And then I answered.

"*West Side Story.*"

Darla actually jumped up and down like a child about to

get their dream Christmas present. Then, her excited shouting morphed into reverence. "I just *love West Side Story*. My mom used to play it for me on her CD player when I was a little girl. We'd dance to 'I Feel Pretty,' around the living room while my dad sat on the couch and laughed at us. Once I even convinced my brother to learn the duet with me—the one with Maria and Anita, you know?" She searched my eyes for recognition, but I just shook my head.

"Don't ever tell him I told you that—he'd be so embarrassed! So, you don't know the musical at all?" she asked.

"Nah. I don't really think I know any, actually," I answered, racking my brain for any scraps of knowledge pertaining to musicals. Nothing. My dad was more into rock, and my mom had loved classical.

"You'll love it! I can't wait for tryouts! Oh, my gosh, Ollie, I could kiss you right now!" she exclaimed.

Wait, what? I felt a sudden warmth in my ears, my face flushed, and I silently prayed my nervousness didn't show. But Darla could definitely tell something had changed.

"Oh, no, I didn't mean—I'm sorry," she rambled. "I wasn't trying to say you'd want, well, you know—it's an expression. Sort of," she continued, twisting her bracelet.

"Yeah—no—whatever," I added ever so eloquently, waving it off with the back of my hand. All I could think of now was that if Julian were here to witness my awkwardness he would smack me on the back of my head and tell me to stop being an idiot.

"Ok, well, thanks," Darla said, and my heart sank a little, as her enthusiasm had seemed to dissipate. What had just happened exactly?

12
Darla

A few minutes later

"It was *beyond* embarrassing," I mumbled into my hands as I sat back in my seat in the cafeteria.

"What? Stop grumbling, Darla. I can hardly understand you," Harlow said, sounding a bit too much like my mother. I took my head out of my hands and looked at her sheepishly.

"I think I made a complete fool of myself," I admitted.

"With Ollie?" Harlow questioned a little too loudly while pointedly looking in his direction.

"Stop looking over there!" I whispered frantically, pulling her arm back toward me. "What if he sees you staring? He'll know we're talking about him!"

"Darla, slow down and start from the beginning. I'm sure it's not that bad."

Easy for her to say. I explained to Harlow how I told

Ollie I could just kiss him, and the look on his face was similar to if I had asked him to stomp on a worm and eat it—horror mixed with disgust. *Yes, that's what it was. Definitely.* Harlow just vigorously shook her head.

"No," she stated very matter-of-factly, again sounding like my mom.

"What do you mean, 'No'?"

"No," she repeated. "You read it wrong. You probably caught him off-guard or something—who knows what goes on inside the mind of a teenage boy? And don't take offense, but Darla, you are a teensy-weensy bit melodramatic."

"*What?*" I inhaled a deep breath in shock, placing my hand to my chest. *Alright. Maybe she had a point.*

"Ollie totally likes you," she continued. I was about to protest when she put a hand up to stop me and continued. "He always waits for you after class, walks you to your locker after school, finds reasons to pass you notes in algebra!" she persisted until she was satisfied that I believed her.

Except I didn't.

The inflection of Harlow's voice conveyed slight agitation as she continued, "Darla—he goes to the pet shop every night to see you . . . at work no less." As if *that* were definitive proof.

I could see what she was saying. But it was one thing to think or hope he liked me. It was another thing to actually *believe* it. "Sometimes he buys dog food?" I offered as a lame rebuttal, but even as I said it, I realized that Harlow was right and I was overreacting. I stole a glance across the cafeteria, and sure enough, Ollie caught my stare and smiled.

13
Julian

The next week

The first time I skipped school with Liam and Pete, we went to a run-down-looking arcade. I was surprised at first; it seemed too *juvenile* for Liam. But after arriving, we headed to the back to a billiards room, where we each threw in ten bucks for a game. Liam grabbed the triangle, racked, broke, and sank two balls, informing me that my $10 was as good as gone.

The time after that, we'd gone to this huge pier and went fishing. It was open to the public and had a steady stream of fishermen, even for the middle of the week, when you'd think most people would be at work . . . *or school.*

Another time we paid someone to sneak us into Dodger Stadium. Apparently they give tours in the off-season. Ollie would have loved seeing the inside of the stadium. It has a seating capacity over fifty thousand. I didn't tell him about it, though. Not sure how he would react to my being there—on a school day.

I found myself going to school less and less and spending more and more money. I'd blown nearly half of the funds I'd saved from working at the deli. On top of that, I was getting worried about midterm exams. My dad would never let me stay in California if my grades ended up worse than they were back home. Exams weren't that far away, but every time I asked Liam about how he planned on passing, he just laughed and told me not to worry.

Today our activities were a little different than usual. Instead of cutting school to hang out, Pete and Liam gave me an address, where I was supposed to meet them that night. They didn't tell me what we were doing, so I was highly suspicious when the address turned out to be a convenience store. It was way past dusk, giving everything an eerie feel. I could see, *and smell*, trash everywhere: cans, bottles, and cardboard boxes were strewn in piles along the walkway, spilling into the street. There were several homeless people, too, in the less populated streets, sitting on sleeping bags or folding chairs. Some had signs that read things like, "*Anything helps.*"

My Aunt Sarah definitely wouldn't have liked me being in this part of town at night, so I avoided the problem by simply not telling her. She was a nurse, and tonight she was working a late shift. I'd make it back home before she knew I'd even left.

I waited impatiently outside of the convenience store, checking my watch every few minutes. *They're late.* I checked inside the store, too, but there was no sign of them—just a few customers buying booze. *Alright, back to pacing out front, I guess.* The weather was surprisingly cool, but I couldn't say it was exactly pleasant with the air smelling like a mixture of old deli meat. My watch read 9:40. I'd give them ten minutes; then, I'd leave.

The convenience store was the only shop on this street, and its fluorescent lighting was the only source of light in the area (there seemed to be no working street lamps), so when I saw four silhouettes approaching me from down the street, my heart began to race. I began cracking my knuckles subconsciously, a bad habit of mine when a little on edge.

When the figures got close, I could finally make out that one was Liam and breathed a small sigh of relief. Then I recognized Pete. The guy behind Liam had his face mostly obscured by a dark hoodie, so I wasn't sure who he was. And the other one, with a mop of dark curly hair and a small goatee, looked older than we were, maybe eighteen or so. I'd never seen him before, for sure.

"Julian," Liam said with a nod hello, drawing out my name so it sounded more like Joo-lian. "Are you ready to have some fun?"

Honestly? I didn't know. I couldn't shake the uneasy feeling that had lodged itself in the pit of my stomach.

"Who are your friends?" I asked suspiciously. Liam gave a small laugh. "Don't worry about them," he said with too much emphasis, making him sound like a sleazy car salesman you might see on a TV show.

"Yeah, I don't know if I'm up to hanging out tonight," I started. Liam quickly put his arm around my shoulder and pulled me slightly away from Pete and the two others.

"Relax, Dude. These are my brothers. We are only going downtown a little ways from here. Come on—don't let me down.

I told them how cool you were. Don't make me look bad."

I wasn't sure if I believed Liam, but I decided to go with the flow. *That's always a good idea, right?*

We walked for what seemed like forever, the streets getting darker and less populated.

"Here. This is good," Goatee Guy said.

"Heaven spot, man," Hoodie nodded in reverence, like he'd stumbled across something magical or holy. I had no idea what he meant, so I just stood there looking at the building we were in front of—a large brick apartment complex with an old fire escape running down the side.

It was only then that I realized Goatee Guy was wearing a black backpack, or at least it looked black at night. He started to climb the fire escape.

"What's he doing?" *And why are we all just standing around watching?*

"Street art." Pete answered.

"You mean graffiti?" I asked.

"Yeah, and it's a felony, so be on the lookout," Hoodie Guy said gruffly. I looked around furtively and didn't see a soul. Even the apartment building looked empty. Perhaps it was abandoned?

I watched as Goatee Guy shook a can of paint up above, the rattling sound piercing the otherwise quiet night. He glanced below to Hoodie, who gave a nod of approval. Approving what, I wasn't sure. *The spot he chose? Or that it was ok to start?* I could hear the sound of the spray can and see some white splatter against a brick wall. He moved quickly, and methodically, making large block letters. It looked like, "MARK 10:27."

"Is that his name, Mark?" I asked. The three guys all

began to laugh simultaneously. I didn't mind Pete and Liam so much, but Hoodie pissed me off, as the guy didn't know me well enough—or at all—to justify laughing. It was more like ridicule in my mind. My eyes darted in his direction with a glare, when Liam spoke up.

"No, that's his tag."

"That's like a signature, right?" I asked again, not caring if Hoodie had something to say about my ignorance.

"Yeah, something like that," Liam nodded with a smirk. Now *he* was beginning to get on my nerves.

"Then why sign the name 'Mark' if that's not his name?" Might as well keep asking questions. There was nothing else to do while Goatee finished up his "art." Surprisingly, it was Hoodie that answered.

"It's from the Bible. It means, 'with God, all things are possible,'" he said in a tone that was daring to ask me another question. But I didn't. I couldn't help myself—I laughed instead. *Yeah, we are definitely not going to be friends.*

"What's so funny about the Bible?" Hoodie said, taking a few strides toward me, his eye squinting.

"Leave it alone, Sebastian," Liam quickly said. He made a move to step between us, but Hoodie/Sebastian was already standing too close to my face for Liam to get in between. He was so close I could see his nostrils flaring.

"I don't know, actually." I stood my ground and kept my tone casual. No way would I let this guy intimidate me. "I don't know anything about the Bible, but I thought people who believed in God were supposed to be, I don't know, righteous? Definitely not criminals."

"For someone who doesn't know anything about the

Bible, you sure have a big mouth about it," Sebastian continued, leaning in closer to my face with every word he spoke. Although there was barely any room between us, I was feeling bold and took a step closer.

"Well? Am I wrong? Isn't it hypocritical for you to break the law by defacing public property with a . . . Bible quote?" I asked.

"It's called *scripture*, genius. And believing in God isn't about being righteous. It's knowing you are forgiven even though you're not."

"Hate the sin and love the sinner!" Pete sang out, in a weak attempt to be funny and break the tension. I ignored his outburst and kept looking at Sebastian.

"Well, since I don't know anything about your *art* or the Bible, I guess I'll have to take your word." I hoped he got the dig about the word "art." Judging by the murderous look in his eye, I'd safely bet he did.

"Yeah, you do that," he spat, but still didn't take a step back. The rickety fire escape came to life again with a squeal, and we all turned to see Goatee jump safely to the ground, backpack in hand.

"Let's go," he said, and the three other guys all turned to follow like obedient, loyal dogs. I stayed put. This wasn't my scene. It wasn't fun. But could I just leave on my own? Liam turned to look at me and saw my hesitation.

"You coming or not?" he asked sharply. Maybe I embarrassed him. I didn't want to lose the only friend I had here, so I had to make a choice.

"Yeah. I'm coming."

14
Oliver

The next day

"I think I lost Percy!" Darla nearly screamed as she opened the Pet Palace door, pulling me inside by my sweatshirt, then quickly locking the door behind me. I decided to come by before the store opened to bring her an apple turnover that Hannah made and a cup of her favorite Rooibos tea. I did not expect crazed panic. I don't do well with panic.

"Who's Percy?" I asked as Darla dragged me past the fish and bird aisle over to the rodent section of the store.

"A pup," she answered, dropping my arm and stopping in front of the rodent cages, an empty glass one sitting on the floor. I tilted my head as if I'd heard her wrong.

"You lost a puppy?" I asked in disbelief. *How does someone lose a puppy indoors?* Darla shook her head frantically, pointing to the empty cage on the floor.

"No, not a dog. A baby mouse. They're called pups. The mom is here," she explained, pointing with a shaky finger toward a different cage with a plump, greyish brown rodent with ears too big for its body. "That's Molly. And she had seven pups, so naturally I named them Bill, Charlie, Percy, Fred, George, Ron and Ginny."

"Yeah, naturally," I agreed. I didn't have a clue what she was talking about. Darla ran her hands though her hair, which she had worn down today, and sighed. It was always such a contrast to see her in khaki pants and the uniform Pet Palace polo, instead of her usual dresses and skirts. But she looked pretty no matter what she wore.

"Everyone is accounted for, except Percy. I was cleaning the cage, putting in fresh bedding, and now Percy is gone." Her arms flailed in the air and then fell to her sides in desperation.

"Let me help you." Yeah, that sounded like the right thing to say. After all, how far could a rodent go on its own?

"Here, take these." I thrust the tea and turnover into her hands. "They're from Hannah. I'll start looking."

"Thank you, Ollie!"

"Any chance it fell into the cage below?"

"I guess it's possible *he* fell."

I didn't think this was really the time for her to dwell on pronouns, but I knew for sure it was *definitely* not the time for me to call her out on it.

"There's a cage in the back that was out when I was doing the cleaning. I'll go check it again."

"Ok. You check that one more time while I look around this cage, then we can search around on the floor. Odds are you just overlooked it—er—him." I felt like a horrible person even thinking it, but mice were just rodents, right? Six pups were accounted for. Would it really be that big a deal if she lost one? I decided it was best to keep my opinion to myself on this one.

I dug around the fluffy cedar chips, thankfully clean, avoiding the mouse pile-up in the corner. I'd "sort" through them when I was finished with the first task. Then, something clicked.

"Oh!" I called out.

"You found him?" Darla asked, her head quickly peeking around the corner with a mix of excitement and relief.

"No . . . ah . . . sorry. I just got the name reference. Harry Potter, right?"

Her shoulders slumped and she just turned and went back to looking.

"Darla!" I called out.

"Yes, Ollie, Harry Potter," she shouted impatiently.

"No, no. I mean, I think I see him. Did you check this tunnel?"

She came running over and immediately fell to her knees to see eye level in the cage. A small gasp escaped her lips. "I would have sworn I checked it. More than once!" she said.

"That's him! Yes, thank you, God!" She looked up to the ceiling with her hands clasped as if she were praying. "And thank you, Ollie. I looked all through this cage I don't know how many times. I can't believe I missed him." She closed the cage gingerly. "You little rascal," she scolded the mouse with what seemed to be genuine annoyance. "Seriously, thank you, Ollie. I know it may seem silly. It's just one mouse—"

"Oh, no, I get it," I quickly agreed.

"—and let's face it, mice are little breeding machines,

but still, I couldn't have stopped looking until I found him." Her brown eyes looked up into mine, holding my gaze. I, on the other hand, had a hard time doing the "gaze" thing.

"Anytime," I shrugged, scanning the place, suddenly finding the guinea pig food display quite fascinating.

"So, what brings you in here anyway? And thanks so much for the special delivery!" We finally stood up, and she brushed her hands off on her khaki pants.

"Oh, uh, I just thought I'd say hi," I stuttered. "And Hannah made turnovers," I added, running my fingers through my hair, desperately trying to think of something to say that wouldn't sound lame. "She, uh, thought you'd like one." *Not lame at all, right?*

"And she knows my favorite tea?" Darla asked, a glint in her eye that made me realize she was teasing. She knew full well that I was just using Hannah as an excuse to come over. I wasn't sure how to answer, so I just shrugged and smiled.

"Well, thank you," she said quietly. For a minute we stood there in a peaceful silence. But then it was ruined. "Oh shoot!" she yelled, startling me out of my thoughts. "I only have ten minutes before I have to open, and I need to get these spare cages away and sweep up. Sorry, Ollie," she explained, once again pulling me by my sweatshirt, back to the door to leave.

"Yeah, sure, I'll let you get back to work," I said as if I had a choice. She unlocked the door and I pushed it open. But I couldn't let it go until I came to do what I'd really wanted to do all along.

"Hey Darla?"

"Yeah?" she asked.

"Do you want to go out with me? It doesn't have to be tonight, but maybe on your next night off we can go to the movies or something." I felt an eerie quiet while I waited breathlessly for her to answer. Fortunately, she didn't make me wait long.

"I'd love to."

15
Darla

"So?" Harlow asked open-mouthed as she waited eagerly for me to talk. I knew exactly what she was asking, but I was in a playful mood, so I decided to tease it out of her.

"What are you talking about?" I asked demurely.

"You know *exactly* what I am talking about, Darla! Last night was your first date with Ollie, right? How did it go? Don't you dare hold back on me." She added that last bit with a threatening tone that was surprisingly menacing for someone as tiny as she was. But who was I kidding? My need to tell her everything outweighed my desire to make her wait. I was *dying* to share the details with someone, and quite honestly, I was thrilled she'd asked. If I didn't tell someone soon, I might even have resorted to bursting into song like Maria from *The Sound of Music*.

"It was wonderful," I said in an airy voice, resisting the

urge to throw my arms out wide and shout it for the world to hear—or, well, the students now standing in the way of my locker. I cleared my throat dramatically until the two boys moved so I could get my books for the next class. "We went to Basil's Pizzeria downtown," I finally continued.

"Wow. That sounds . . . actually, that sounds kind of boring. Is that *it*?" She scrunched her features into a frown, making no attempt to hide her disappointment.

"No," I retorted, sticking my tongue out at her. "We were going to see a movie, but there wasn't anything playing either of us wanted to see, so we decided to go bowling."

"Eh, bowling? But it's so *boring* waiting around while someone else takes their turn." I could tell Harlow was quickly losing interest as her gaze started drifting down the hall.

"It wasn't boring. It was *amazing*. We talked about so many things, like our favorite books, movies, and music—obviously music—then we talked about things like our families and hobbies. Did you know our school has a photography club?" I had no idea how into photography Ollie was. Suddenly, like a seasoned stage actress, I swooned, steadying myself against my locker, as thoughts of our date swirled through my mind. I felt the smile on my face growing, remembering how sweet Ollie had been—paying for my meal, always holding the door open for me, asking me all sorts of questions. Harlow shook me out of my contemplation with her sudden interjection.

"Aw, you are so smitten! It's so cute—yet slightly nauseating," she stated. I just shook my head at her, refusing to let her ruin my perfect mood. Rather than continue to defend myself, or my perfect date, I opted to change the subject instead.

"I've gotta be somewhere; I'll have to catch up with you

later," I said as we got to two intersecting halls where we parted ways.

"Fine. But if you left out any good parts of the date, make sure you tell me later. You can leave out the boring stuff, like the stuff you just told me." She dismissed me with a smile and a wave as she bounded down the hall.

#

"Just what do you think you are doing?" a sickeningly sweet voice came from behind me. I turned slowly to find Charlotte Jones, the most popular girl in our grade, standing with her hands on the hips of her designer jeans. I had never had the "pleasure" of talking with her before, but somehow I didn't think this was going to be a friendly conversation. What I was about to do was sign up for the lead role auditions for the Spring Musical. There were four different sign-up sheets on the bulletin board outside of the band room, depending on what kind of role you wanted, or if you wanted to be part of the costume or stage crew team. We only had three more minutes before the next class, so the halls were buzzing as students hurriedly swapped books from their lockers. I stared down at the pen in my hand momentarily, thinking it was pretty obvious what I was doing. But whatever Charlotte planned to do about it, I didn't have a clue.

"I, um, was, a, just—" I stuttered, hating myself for showing weakness. Any girl who survived middle school knew that popular girls never changed; they were sharks, searching for blood in the water, ready to pick a fight with anyone who threatened their status.

"You, um, were, a just, *what*?" she mocked me, laughing

at her own imitation, then flipping her red curls over her shoulder in a dramatic show of superiority. Her group of loyal followers was there as well, laughing behind her in solidarity. Whatever Charlotte did, Ada and Kennedy did, too.

It was sort of funny to see them all with their hands on their hips, flipping their hair, just like Charlotte. I mean, *exactly* like Charlotte. It was like they were robotic clones you'd find in some science fiction movie my brother watched too much of. They gave me the creeps: Ada, Kennedy, *and* the movies. Fighting the fear that had momentarily given me pause, I gathered my courage as quickly as possible; no reason to prolong what I *was* going to do. With my free hand, I smoothed out the non-existent wrinkles from my rose-colored plaid mini-skirt and stood tall.

"I was about to sign up for auditions," I said sweetly.

"I can see that, genius." Her words were biting. "But supporting cast and stage crew signups are over there." She twirled her finger around until it pointed to the other sheets on the bulletin board and raised her eyebrows with a look that dared me to argue. I couldn't believe her nerve! How could she get away with intimidating people like this? I loved singing and acting, but this? She was taking it way too far. I was not going to let her stop me just because she wanted to handpick the cast.

I knew I had to think—and fast. I was never one for confrontation, so I decided to keep playing naïve and put my acting skills to the test. With a small shrug and smile, I explained, "I just thought I'd give the lead a shot. There's probably no way I would actually get it"—I rolled my eyes like the thought of it was absolutely absurd—"but I thought, you know, it would be fun to try."

"Oh, how cute!" she said with enthusiasm. "But don't,"

she finished venomously.

Ok, the shark was coming in for the kill. Clearly, Charlotte *wasn't* one to avoid confrontation. The crowds in the hall were getting scarcer as the next bell neared. Before I could decide what to do next, Charlotte took a small step toward me, her neck outstretched and making a sniffing sound.

"Ada? Kennedy? Do you *smell* that?" Charlotte asked, feigning innocence.

Really? Are they actually going to fall for this? It seemed so; Ada followed her lead immediately, taking a step forward and sniffing the air. Kennedy, like an actress who'd forgotten her lines, lunged forward a second too late, overcompensating for her lag.

"You work at Pet Palace, don't you, Darla?" I knew where this was going before she even opened her mouth, and there wasn't anything I could do about it.

"Yes," I answered confidently—or at least I hoped confidently. I looked around to see how many more witnesses there were to my pending humiliation. *A fair amount.* Some even slowed to witness the spectacle. *Oh, thanks.*

"That's it!" Charlotte exclaimed, like a mathematician who'd just found the last digit of Pi. "That explains the smell! I *thought* I smelled animal feces," she proclaimed, bobbing her head up and down as if all the pieces of an impossible puzzle were coming together at last. "Don't you smell it, Kennedy?" she continued.

"Me? Oh, uh, yeah. Totally. Like soiled rodent bedding," Kennedy contributed with a look of glee. I'm not sure if she was happier about her clever insult or her chance to please Charlotte.

"Darla, from one girl to another, I have to ask . . ."

Charlotte paused, like this was difficult for her to ask. It wasn't. "Do you shower when you come home from work? Wash your clothes, or"—her eyes widened like this was her lightbulb moment—"maybe the stench is in your hair! Do you wash your hair every day? You should really consider it." She added the last part in a near whisper, as if the onlookers couldn't hear every last word.

She was *so* mean—the kind of mean that caused your eyes to sting and your throat to feel like you swallowed a tater tot whole. I knew things about Charlotte's family. I'd heard rumors about how her life wasn't really as perfect as she made it seem. I wanted to make her cringe with embarrassment. I wanted to belt out for all to hear, the rumors I'd heard about why her father *really* traveled all the time. I clenched my fist and considered it—*truly* considered it.

But I also knew the right thing to do.

I let out a deep breath and relaxed my shoulders, trying to release the tension. Anyone who knew anything about the Bible could tell you what Jesus said are the most important commandments: "Love God with all your heart and soul, and love your neighbor as yourself." Pretty clear. I knew that I should treat Charlotte the way I wanted to be treated. But that wasn't what I was hearing in my head right now, which screamed, *Humiliate her! She deserves it for everything she does to hurt others. Who does she think she is anyway?* But in the crevices of my soul, I could hear the echoes of my Sunday School teacher reciting Proverbs 15:1: "A soft answer turns away wrath, but a harsh word stirs up anger."

What would I really accomplish by following Charlotte's poor example? Nothing but getting myself into more trouble.

And what kind of person would that make me? Not one I'd be proud of.

I quickly turned from her before I could chicken out, and signed up for the lead role auditions, right under the only other name on the list—hers. Without giving her another glance, I bolted out of there like a spooked fawn. I ran through the nearly deserted halls and straight into history class, throwing myself into my seat with a huff. I turned to see Ollie staring at me with a look of curiosity.

"What happened to *you*? Your cheeks are all red," he asked.

"I signed up to try out for the role of Maria." Right then, the bell finally rang and the teacher pulled out her attendance book, a clear indicator we were about to begin.

"And that explains you being out of breath, how?" Ollie whispered.

"I'll tell you later," I mouthed. Right now, I needed to calm down and try to focus on class, not to mention cheer victoriously in my head for my small win against Charlotte Jones.

16
Sarah

A few days later

When Julian first arrived at my place, he told me he loved my "apartment." Sigh. I quickly corrected him, explaining natives called this a "beach condo." It might not be much (although you'd never have guessed it based on my mortgage payment), but it was mine, and I loved every one of the one-thousand square feet of it. It wasn't easy living on your own in a place by the beach, but I was lucky to find this condo and lucky my nursing job kept me employed.

It was a bit of an adjustment giving up one of only two bedrooms to my nephew (not to mention relocating my rarely used elliptical and mounds of nursing textbooks), but it was worth it to have him here. Ever since I'd moved to the west coast, I saw my family less and less. And when my sister died . . . well, even less than that.

My place was in a small community of condos. It had a beautifully renovated kitchen with a grey granite countertop—but its narrow configuration left no room for a full-sized table, or any table at all, actually. Ollie and I, when we ate together, either sat at the island, big enough for two, or on the couch. My place also had a cute balcony (I was on the second floor), overlooking a parking lot and other condos. What it lacked in view, it made up for with its easy access to the fresh California air that took my mind off of the hustle and bustle of work.

I sat out there in my foldable camping chair, biting my nails while reading some missed texts from my brother-in-law, Keith. Christmas was just weeks away, and I didn't know how to tell Julian he wasn't going back home to Virginia—not that he said he wanted to go anyway. The price of a plane ticket was just too expensive. I guess I would just have to do my best to make Christmas memorable here. Maybe I could cook a special meal or something.

With newfound optimism, I lifted myself out of my flimsy chair and went back inside to tell Julian the *good* news.

"Hey," I started. "Texting Ollie?" Julian wasn't the kind of kid to stay glued to his phone, so when he was locked onto a screen, I just assumed he was talking to his brother.

"Reading an email he sent me," he replied politely, but keeping his eyes on the phone. "He has a girlfriend," he added, almost as an afterthought. I detected a measure of surprise in his voice.

"Really? Do you know who it is?" Curiosity grabbed ahold of me like a rubbernecker on a California freeway.

"I don't *really* know her. I saw her a few times," he said with a strange smile.

Hmm. That was intriguing. I fought the urge to ask. *Who was I kidding?*

"Dare I ask?" I prodded.

"Probably best if you don't," he replied with a growing smirk. I shook my head, recognizing defeat when presented with it. But to my surprise, Julian kept talking.

"She seems nice, though. She actually got Ollie to dress up in something other than a t-shirt and made him go to church."

"Now *there* is a sight to see. I hope your dad got a picture." I smiled at the idea of seeing Ollie all grown up with a girlfriend and going to church. The comment, however, earned me a sideways glance from Julian, like I had just told him the Easter Bunny was real and he had the awkward job of breaking the news to me that it wasn't. I guess Keith wasn't one for cameras. It made sense. It had always been Anna taking on that role when she was alive. God, I missed my sister.

"So, you guys never go to church? Not even on Christmas or Christmas Eve?" I started my investigation of Christmas do's and don'ts. It would be our first holiday together in a long time.

"Why would we?" he asked as if the idea were as foreign as taking a cat on a walk with a leash.

"Well, I know *you* celebrate Christmas, and it's a religious holiday. Didn't Anna ever take you to church?" I moved closer to him, perching myself on the arm of the small leather couch he sat on.

He pondered for a minute, then answered, "Maybe. A few times, I think. But it wasn't like it was part of our normal holiday traditions or anything. Why? Do you go to church?"
I decided to give Julian the short answer to this complicated

question. We were still in the get-to-know-you-again stage of our relationship and I didn't want to unburden on him. "No, but I used to. Your mother and I both grew up going to church."

"Why did she stop?" he asked with genuine curiosity. I was glad he liked talking about his mom and didn't avoid the subject. I was also grateful he'd asked about his mom's church attendance and not mine.

"I'm not exactly sure," I answered truthfully. "I don't think it was a conscious choice *not* to go; more likely she just slowly stopped making it a priority. And your dad, of course, isn't a believer. Some people turn to God after things they see and experience in war, like he did. But others—they turn away."

"So why did *you* stop going?"

Oh. How could I tell my nephew I had lost my faith and was still making an effort to gain it back? I knew there was a God. But believing in God and trusting in Him were two different things. When my boyfriend of four years broke up with me after nursing school, I was devastated. I started questioning all of my life choices. And then, when Anna died soon after? I was beyond crushed. That was when I started questioning a whole lot more. My heart was finally healing, but I was a work-in-progress, with the help from my ever-vigilant friend, Audrey. She liked to remind me that faith was not the absence of doubt; it was trusting even in doubt's presence. *And speaking of Audrey . . .*

"How about we talk about that another time? My friend Audrey is going to be here soon. Are you sure you don't mind if we hang out in the living room? I just assumed you were going over to your friend's house tonight. Otherwise I wouldn't have invited her."

"Nah, I don't mind. As long as you don't mind me hanging out in my bedroom. I'll probably get some homework out of the way."

"Sounds perfect. So, Julian, about Christmas . . ." Better to get the seed planted now, I reasoned.

"I don't want to go home," he stated rather abruptly but then quickly added, "if that's ok with you?"

"Oh. Ok, of course." I hoped I sounded cheery enough so he knew his presence was welcome, but I couldn't mask the surprise I felt from his reaction. Before I could say anything else, though, I heard a knock on the front door. I guess that problem was solved. But it sure didn't feel like it was.

17

Julian

A moment earlier

"So, Julian, about Christmas," my aunt asked, trying to be non-chalant, but I could tell by the way she was biting her fingernails that this was something that had been worrying her. And I could guess why. I'd known when my father told me I could spend one school year out here in California that traveling back and forth wasn't going to be feasible. We'd skirted the issue of holidays, but I think we both knew what me coming out here meant. I decided to put Aunt Sarah out of her misery.

"I don't want to go home." The words shot out of my mouth, surprising even me by their forcefulness. But then, for the first time, I considered that *she* might have other plans. *Oh, crap.* Guilt started to build quickly. "If that's ok with you?" I asked with quiet hope.

"Oh. Ok, of course," she answered, straightening her

posture as if a spotlight were suddenly shining upon her. I could tell she was surprised I didn't want to go home. *Please don't ask me to share my feelings.* But I was saved by a knock at the door. Aunt Sarah swung her legs over the arm of the couch and bounced excitedly to the door.

"I brought Sangria," a deep female voice crooned, holding each syllable of her words like they were song lyrics, and waving a bottle in the air. Before I was asked to make small talk, I grabbed my phone and headed to my room, hoping my slight, polite smile and wave could replace formalities.

I was taking a break from hanging out with Liam and Pete, but as soon as I entered my room, my phone beeped; a text. I looked down to read a message from Liam, not sure if I was relieved or more worried than before.

> Hey bro! Remember talking about
> passing midterm exams?

Yeah, of course.

> Well, it's time.

To what?

> Study :)

> We have a way to get all the answers
> we need on the standardized tests.
> Teachers have to create answer
> keys and submit them to the
> principal. Mr. Mahoney, the janitor,
> will slip me the key to the office

where they keep the answer keys.

So, what, u need me to go with u for this?

Oh no. Mr. Mahoney only deals with me. He gets itchy when other people r around. What we need is incentive.

You pay him?

Of course!

So, what do u need from me?

Not much. Just $300.

$300?! Please tell me u mean $100 from each of us?

No man. $300 each . . . r u good with that?

Was I? If I gave Liam $300, that would be it—I wouldn't have any money left from the deli. All my savings—gone. I could hear my dad's voice in my head saying how irresponsible I was. But if I didn't do this, there was no way I'd pass my sophomore year of high school. My dad would be beyond angry. I'd be forced to go home and have even less of a life than I did before. But did I even trust Liam? He acted like he'd done this before, but his judgment might not be something I'd want to bet my future on. Really, at this point, what choice did I have?

Yeah, I'm good. I'll pay u tomorrow at school.

18
Darla

One day later

Favorite charcoal grey, pleated skirt? *Check.*

Favorite black leggings and boots? *Double check.*

Lucky light-grey scoop-neck blouse? *Check, check, check!*

Today was the day of my audition with the director of the Spring Musical, aka Mr. Wood, the school's drama teacher. I had rehearsed my song for weeks, non-stop, to the point where even my brother could recite the lyrics (to his embarrassment) and my mother banned it from the house. I was ready!

After school, I headed straight to the band room with confidence, sheet music in hand and head held high. One thing I'd learned from other auditions at schools and camps was that attitude is a huge part of success. If you believe you can, *you can.* But just in case, I'd also said a prayer last night (ok, that morning, too) that God would grant me the courage I needed.

When I got to the band room, the lights were out. *That's odd.* Maybe I was too early?

I checked my paper again, and I definitely had the right time. I decided just to wait, so I took a seat at an empty desk in the front of the room. I began reading the posters on the wall, almost involuntarily, about stage positioning and styles of musical theatre. That was when Charlotte walked in with a wide smile plastered on her face like a Barbie Doll.

"Oh, hey Darla! What brings you here?" she practically snorted, like she was trying to hold in a laugh.

Oh, no.

"My audition," I replied, with what I hoped was a knowing look in my eyes. She didn't fool me. I *knew* something was wrong and it was her fault.

Her face contorted to a sad face with a pouty bottom lip. "Oh, no! I'm *so* sorry!" she began, innocently twisting her red braid between her fingers. "Auditions were yesterday. Didn't you get your confirmation?" Charlotte was back to grinning, and I was seething mad.

"What–did–you–*do*?" I annunciated each word with hatred. Charlotte dropped all pretense of innocence at this point and glowered at me.

"Nothing you can prove," she answered calmly. Quickly, I mentally reviewed everything I knew about the audition. I did have the right day and time; I was sure of it. My homeroom teacher, Ms. Gibson, had handed the confirmation slip to me; I had no doubt. So where did Ms. Gibson get it from? Mr. Wood. And who did he give the slips to in order to deliver to homerooms? Of course. It had to have been Charlotte or one of her friends. I stood up slowly, with as much dignity as I could, and doing my best impersonation of an angry Mob Boss, I simply stated, "This isn't over."

I walked past her, giving her an icy stare. She snickered. Not exactly the reaction I was going for; I was at least hoping to see a flicker of fear in her eyes, but *whatever*. I meant what I said, and I wouldn't go down without a fight. Since I'd already missed the bus, I walked home as fast as I could and immediately took out my laptop to email Mr. Wood.

To: LWood@shhs.org
December 5
Subject: Musical Audition

Hi Mr. Wood,
There seems to have been some confusion over my audition slot. I received my note that it was Friday, not Wednesday. Can I audition sometime next week? Any day will work for me.

Thanks,
Darla Green

To: DarlaGreen@shhs.org
December 5
Subject: Re: Musical Audition

Hi Darla,
I'm afraid I was very clear that we do not have time for

make-up auditions, which is why I asked everyone to let me know asap if they could not make it. The lead has already been cast, but I would encourage you to join the stage crew. We have several slots available, and you'll find it is a very rewarding experience.

Best,
Mr. Wood

To: LWood@shhs.org
December 6
Subject: Re: Re: Musical Audition

Hi Mr. Wood,
Sorry to bother you again, but I really, REALLY want a singing role. I showed up on the day my paper said to be there. I think I am the victim of sabotage. Please, please, please let me audition! I can come before or after school. Or study hall.

Thank you for your consideration,
Darla

To: DarlaGreen@shhs.org
December 8
Subject: Re: Re: Re: Musical Audition

Hi Darla,

I'm sure sabotage was not in play here. Consider this a learning experience and try your best to honor your commitments in the future. Remember, you are only a sophomore and have two more years ahead to take part in the annual musical. I look forward to working with you then.

Mr. Wood

To: LWood@shhs.org
December 9
Subject: Re: Re: Re: Re: Musical Audition

Hi Mr. Wood,
Did you get the chocolate muffins I made you yesterday? I hope you do not have any food allergies. I just wanted you to know that I have been practicing songs from the musical just in case you reconsider allowing me to audition. I have memorized them.

Thanks,
Darla

To: DarlaGreen@ shhs.org
December 10
Subject: Re: Re: Re: Re: Re: Musical Audition

Yes, Darla, I received the muffins. I shared them in the Teachers' Lounge and they were most appreciated.

To: LWood@shhs.org
December 11
Subject: Re: Re: Re: Re: Re: Re: Musical Audition

Hi Mr. Wood,
I think I have a solution to our problem! Perhaps you can let me sing for you, but it doesn't have to be an "official" audition. I worked REALLY hard on my piece, and it seems a waste not to have the opportunity to get your critique. Does after school work for you?

To: LWood@shhs.org
December 11
Subject: Re: Re: Re: Re: Re: Re: Musical Audition

Hi Mr. Wood,
I didn't hear back from you regarding my unofficial-audition proposal. I will stop by the band room after school unless I hear otherwise.

Thank you so much for this opportunity! You will not regret it!

When the last bell rang for the day, I ran straight to the drama room, not even bothering to look back to say good-bye to my friends. Mr. Wood taught band last period, so I wanted to catch him there before he had a chance to go to the auditorium for musical rehearsal. When I got to the classroom, there were a few straggling students still packing up their instruments and chatting with each other.

"Hi Mr. Wood!" I called out, simultaneously dropping my book bag on an empty desk, as if I belonged there. *Anything to make it harder for him to boot me out.*

"Darla. I appreciate your enthusiasm, but rules are rules, and it wouldn't be fair to the other students if I broke them just for one person," he pleaded with me from behind his desk. His stern blue eyes behind silver, wire-framed glasses gave me a distinct look of pity, mixed with a good amount of annoyance. I can't say I blamed him, but he didn't know the real story.

"You mean it wouldn't be fair to *Charlotte*," I explained, trying to keep the venom out of my voice. "She is the only one who wouldn't want me to audition. She didn't want *anyone* to audition. Don't you think it's strange that I was the only other person to sign up?" I questioned as delicately as I could. My mom had warned me to be polite. "*You'll catch more flies with honey than with vinegar*" was one of her favorite mottos.

"Darla, it isn't nice to make accusations about people. I made it—"

"Mr. Wood, please," I cut in. "I just want to sing my song. That's it. Please. Just three minutes, and I promise I won't send you any more emails, or show up after class—"

"Or leave me bribes?" he said with a smirk.
I channeled my inner Scarlet O'Hara, pretending to be offended at the suggestion.

"Those weren't *bribes*. Just thank-you's for your consideration." He shook his head and sighed heavily in defeat. *YES! I did it! I wore him down!*

"Three minutes?" I asked sweetly.

"Fine. Three minutes. Go."

Talk about pressure. There were still two students in the band room, clearly interested in our conversation. They'd even sat back down to watch the proceedings. Dismissing their amused stares, I cleared my throat, closed my eyes, and began my acapella performance.

19
Sarah

Mid-December

The dreaded snooze button. I blamed *it* for the horrible day that just seemed to get worse with every hour that went by. It started off with my cell phone alarm buzzing its annoyingly chipper song at 5:45 a.m. (a song I chose, thinking it would put a smile on my face when it rang. It did not). I hit the snooze button, knowing life would be better with an extra ten minutes of sleep, cocooned in my plush lavender comforter. It was not. Nor was it better after 30 minutes, having hit the snooze button two more times.

I finally left the warmth of my bed, only to discover that Julian was in the only shower in my place. *Ugh.* There was no way I had time to get in there before work. *No problem,* I told myself. A little dry shampoo, throw my hair in a bun, put on some clean scrubs, and no one would ever know.

After getting dressed, I made my coffee, then proceeded to spill the coffee down the front of my favorite lilac scrubs. Besides the fact that the coffee practically scalded me, I couldn't find another clean pair of scrubs anywhere in my room. Well, that wasn't entirely true. I did have another clean pair with flamingos and donuts on them that someone once gave me as a joke. But I wouldn't rest until I found another, more dignified, pair.

Ten minutes later, I was sitting in traffic, wearing my flamingo and donut scrubs.

I arrived at work twenty minutes late, which was definitely not appreciated by Patty, the night shift nurse whom I was relieving. She gave me my patient updates and then made a point of saying how she would have to rush home. *Darn snooze button.*

I started with my morning routine, doing some blood work, administering meds, and monitoring the blood sugar of my one diabetes patient. Things picked up before afternoon rounds, so I skipped lunch to catch up on charting, devouring a granola bar to keep me going.

There weren't many new patients coming into the hospital, so I clung to the hope that maybe my day would get better. *Wrong.* While sitting in the break room, I was paged to the nurses' station. So, cramming the last bit of my granola bar into my mouth, I stood up and gathered my paperwork.

"What's up?" I asked my friend, Constance, while approaching the station.

"You have a call," she answered cheerily.

I picked up the phone and pressed the blinking light. "This is Sarah."

"Hi, Sarah, this is Principal Delarosa from Julian's school. How are you today?"

Terrible, now. There was no way this was going to be good news. Suddenly worried that Julian might be hurt or sick, I replied with a brisk "Great, and you?"

"Doing well," he replied quickly, then continued, "but I'm afraid I need you to come to the school as soon as you can to pick up Julian."

"Pick him up? Is he ok?" Panic began to spread. I snatched my hand away from my mouth when I caught myself about to bite my fingernails. *I've got to stop doing that.*

"He's fine, he's fine . . ." Mr. Delarosa tried to sound reassuring. "But there was a situation at school today. I think it's best if you come here to talk in person."

No, no, no. Nothing good ever came from a conversation that was best to have "in person."

"I can be there in thirty minutes, but please, tell me what this is about?" I asked, now nervously fiddling with the ties on my scrubs.

With a brief pause, like a doctor about to give an unwelcome diagnosis, he answered, "Julian has been expelled for the school year."

"Expelled?" I shrieked, startling Constance. A look of alarm spread across her face, which I'm sure mirrored how I felt.

"Sarah, are you sure you wouldn't rather come here—"

"No, please tell me the basic details," I insisted. There was no way I could drive over there now with a million ideas swimming around in my head, each one undoubtedly worse than the previous.

"Basically? He cheated on his midterm exams."

Oh, no, Julian. What were you thinking? But expulsion?

"Mr. Delarosa, are you sure expulsion is really the solution for cheating on a test?"

"He didn't cheat on *a* test, Sarah," the principal began.
I did not like the way he emphasized the word "a."
"He cheated on *all* of them."
I liked the emphasis on "all" even less.

"H–how?" I stuttered. I couldn't even form a proper thought, let alone a sentence.

"He paid someone to steal the answers from a locked filing cabinet in the school. Sarah—this is serious. He technically could be charged with a crime here, but we really don't want to do that."
No, we definitely didn't want that here either. What was Keith going to do? What was he going to think? And poor Julian. Was this somehow my doing? A flood of emotions rushed over me and I didn't know what to do. Well, I guess I knew the first thing.

"I'm on my way."

20
Darla

To: DarlaGreen@shhs.org
December 15
Subject: West Side Story

Darla,
Please show up to musical rehearsal after school, from 3pm to 5pm.

Well done on your unofficial-audition!
Mr. Wood

I couldn't believe it. Did this mean I'd gotten a part? I really wanted the lead, but at this point, I would have settled for anything. I stared at the email on my phone while sitting in the cafeteria, ignoring my turkey sandwich before me, too stunned to eat.

"What has you going on a hunger strike?" a familiar voice said from behind me. I turned to see Ollie coming my way. He grabbed a seat from the table next to mine, swinging it around to sit backwards on it, arms resting on its hard, plastic back.

"Huh?" I asked, still a bit wrapped up in my own thoughts.

"You haven't touched your food, and you've been staring at your phone for the last five minutes," he explained.
Ever since Ollie and I had gone out together, he started joining us at our lunch table a couple of times a week, sitting with his baseball friends the other times. Today, he sat with them, but he must have been looking over here at me. I felt a twinge of excitement that he'd noticed.

"Aw, how sweet. Your *boyfriend* is worried about you," Harlow said in a mocking voice, while pecking at the French fries on her lunch tray. I could strangle her right now and hoped my dirty look in her direction let her know that. Ollie and I had never "said" we were boyfriend and girlfriend. We went out on a few dates, but did that make it official? I'd talked to Harlow about this before, so this was her way of mocking my insecurity. *Nice friend.* Fortunately, Ollie just laughed off Harlow's teasing and kept his eyes on me.

"So? What's going on?" he continued.

"I got an email from Mr. Wood. He told me to be at play practice today. I think I got a part."

"I knew you would," he said, grabbing and squeezing my hand. Then he left it there on top of mine, and I was jittery for a whole new reason.

A stream of students flowed into the large auditorium after school, sitting down in the scarlet, fixed seats in the front two rows. Large overhead lights were turned on, filling the empty stage and orchestra pit with a soft glow. I followed suit, walking down the carpeted aisles, glancing behind me at the empty balcony seats, reveling in the size and beauty of the theatre. I was jolted out of my reverie when a shrill voice filled my head.

"Are you lost?" Charlotte asked. *Of course* she would single me out before I'd even had a chance to talk to Mr. Wood and find out what I was doing here. What if he really did just want to offer me a stage job? I shook my head, dismissing the idea, but Charlotte read the gesture as if I were responding to her.

"What? Can't speak? And you expected an actual part in the musical?" she snickered.

"I'm here to see Mr. Wood," I said flatly. I didn't feel like quibbling with Charlotte today. Or ever. It wasn't who I was. She just had to accept that.

I walked past her and took an empty seat. I thought that would be the end of it until she spun on her heels and started walking toward me. Thankfully, any further confrontation was avoided with the sudden sound of a booming voice.

"Hey guys?" shouted Mr. Wood, walking briskly up a small side stairway and standing center stage so we all could see him. "Listen up," he called again even louder, and the sound of chatter dwindled like a decrescendo.

"Take a seat," he said, then clapped twice in a gesture

my mom liked to use with a simultaneous *"chop chop,"* to make us hurry. "I'd like to get started. As you know, we spent the first couple of rehearsals reading lines and learning basic melodies. I want to move quickly so we can get as much done as possible before winter break. That said, I do want to make a couple of casting changes. We have two lead female roles, where we need powerful voices. First, Maria."

Charlotte smirked at me with a head tilt that silently said, *"That's me."*

Mr. Wood continued, "and then we have Anita." He gave Deidre Johnson a slight nod, indicating that she must have been cast into that role. To my surprise, Deirdre gave a shy smile in return, almost a look of embarrassment. "Deidra was kind enough to try and step into the role of Anita, but," he paused to say it delicately, "Deidra really doesn't seem thrilled with singing solos."

Ah. That explains her reaction.

"That's ok, Mr. Wood, you can say it. I'm more cut out for the chorus!" she called out, earning her a laugh from the crowd.

"Well, we have a new addition to our cast! Everyone, meet our new Maria . . . Darla Green!"

"Wait, *what?*" two surprised voices called out at the same time—Charlotte's and mine.

"But she missed her audition!" Charlotte continued, actually stomping her foot on the floor like a petulant child.

"Charlotte, I think the alto part of Anita is much better for your vocal range. You'll find you'll be struggling a lot less to get some of those high notes," Mr. Wood explained kindly, but the expression on Charlotte's face looked like he'd just told her she had the voice of sick toad on its death bed.

Charlotte still fuming, Mr. Wood separated us into groups based on what we needed to do for the day, then walked off the stage, back toward the seats that were quickly being vacated by the students. Before I joined my group, which unfortunately included Charlotte, Mr. Wood gave me a small pat on the shoulder.

"You are a very talented girl, Darla, and I'm glad you didn't give up on the musical," he said, then walked hurriedly away to the next task at hand.

WEATHER ALERT: Major Winter Storm Rips Through North Carolina, Making its way to Virginia

Staff Reporter, PAF NEWS

SUGAR HOLLOW— Meteorologists are tracking a major winter storm that has moved through North Carolina and is currently headed toward Virginia.

The National Weather Service has issued a winter storm warning for most of North Carolina. Hundreds have already been left with power outages due to the wet, heavy snow mix, weighing down trees and power lines.

While some Virginia counties are already under a winter weather advisory, Sugar Hollow is only expected to see a wintery mix over the next two days, possibly avoiding the full force of the storm.

Dr. Lawrence Fletcher, meteorologist with the Virginia Weather Commission, forecasts that Sugar Hollow could see 3–8 inches of snow, with higher amounts possible.

21
Harlow

January

With Christmas break behind us and a new year just starting, I had to say—I was *so done* with snow. It was always hit or miss in Virginia as far as snowstorms were concerned; some years we were lucky to get one good sledding snow, while other years we were bombarded with wintery wetness. This holiday, we'd been blessed with a white Christmas. Then we had a white New Year's Eve, white New Year's Day, and a white week before school started again. Luckily (insert eye-roll here) the snow gave us a brief reprieve just in time for us to return to school.

Unable to really travel anywhere over break (not that my family had big plans other than visiting my grandparents just twenty minutes away), things went from fun and exciting, to relaxing, then to boring as fast as a snowflake melts on the palm of your hand. We did have one great sledding snow before the holidays, though. Stacia (and her brother Derrick), Tracy, Kathy, Penn (and her boyfriend Ethan), Ollie, Darla, and I all met up at this gigantic hill just south of town where all the kids went sledding. It ended up more of a snowball fight, boys against girls, but it was awesome. The girls kicked butt, of course.

But now that school was back in session, I was actually kind of glad for something to do. Third period bell rang, and I pushed my way through a crowd of dawdling kids (I'm short—they never knew what hit them until it was too late. *Literally*.). Many of my fellow students sported what were obviously brand-new sweaters and fleeces, another constant reminder of the cold, wet misery that waited just outside.

As I approached Darla and Ollie, I could see Darla fingering the locket Ollie had given her for Christmas. I guess they "officially" labeled themselves girlfriend and boyfriend over break. They were cute as far as couples went—not the annoying flirty ones that always held hands in the already crowded hallway as if they were on a leisurely stroll through the park.

They walked side by side as I neared, and then I abruptly wedged my way between them.

"Did you hear about the blizzard that hit North Carolina this weekend?" I asked the pair.

"Yeah," Ollie stated, only slightly fazed by my sudden appearance. "It's really bad. My uncle lives there and lost power. They have no idea when it will turn back on."

"I didn't know that. That's horrible!" Darla added, with genuine concern. I loved that about her. She was sincere to the core.

"I'll pray for them," she continued. I thought that had ended this first conversation and was on my way to the next—the one about the French teacher getting sick in the cafeteria—when I saw Ollie's expression change to something like a sneer.

"Why are you giving me that look?" Darla asked Ollie with a hesitant smile.

"What look?" Ollie asked.

"The smirk," she continued, still looking as if she were trying to solve an algebra problem on one of Mr. Dubanowski's notorious exams. Ollie just shook his head and gave a small, almost inaudible sigh, as if he were debating what to say.

"It's nothing," he finally spoke. But the "nothing" was obviously "something." I could tell by Darla's expression that she agreed.

"It doesn't *seem* like nothing," she prodded. *Yup. I was right.* This "nothing" wasn't about to go away.

"It's just that, it's sweet that you say you'll pray for them, but it just feels a little . . ." he paused, trying to find the right word. *Good, boy, Ollie. Tread lightly.*

". . . like a platitude?" he finished. *Ugh. Wrong choice, buddy. Abort, Ollie! Abort!* Was I about to witness Darla and Ollie's first fight? I wasn't the only one who grew nervous about Darla's normally sweet disposition becoming a tad more combative. I could see Ollie trying to backtrack a little.

"It's just . . . do you really think praying for them is going to work?" he continued.

"Well—" I tried to interject, but it was futile.

"It depends on what you think the point of prayer is," Darla explained, just a bit defensive. "Praying does a lot of things. One thing is simply that it strengthens your relationship with God," she started. It was clear by her tone that she had more to say on the subject. Well, clear to me, anyway. But Ollie jumped in before she could finish. "Stupid, stupid," I muttered, not meaning to say it out loud. But I did. *Bad habit*. Fortunately (or not), no one paid attention to what *I* was saying.

"So, by you praying for my uncle, you're really only helping yourself? Thanks."

Ouch. That "Thanks" was loaded with enough sarcasm to make Darla flinch. I opened my mouth—yet again—to try to say something to help, but what? This was clearly a touchy subject for both of them. Ollie at least had the good sense to look a little embarrassed after his last comment, but still wasn't looking to capitulate.

"I gotta get something from my locker," he mumbled and turned down the hallway without a good-bye.

"Did you just hear that?" Darla immediately turned to me in outrage.

"Yup."

"Totally crazy reaction, right?" That was a loaded question. In friend code, I knew the emphasis on the word "right" was a clear indication that I was supposed to take her side and condemn Ollie's behavior. I wanted to be a good friend, but in this situation, I didn't think it meant just saying what my friend wanted to hear.

"Nope."

"Um, what?" Darla looked at me like my hair was on fire.

"Darla, you need to take a step back and think about things from Ollie's perspective," I began.

"But he was downright mean about something that not only is important to me but that was meant to be nice," she said aggressively, but I knew only some of the anger was meant ward me—most was still reserved for Ollie.

"I know. And he knows, too. But think about where he is coming from. His mom died just three years ago. How many people probably told him and his family that they would pray for them? How many prayers did he maybe say himself?" That image alone made my eyes sting. "And how did that turn out?" I asked rhetorically. I could tell realization hit Darla like a tsunami; her shoulders relaxed and her eyes now held a look of pity.

"But . . ." she barely whispered, clearly lost for words. Didn't matter.

"I know," I said back. And I did. She didn't mean anything bad. Anyone who knew Darla would never think that. But it didn't mean that Ollie was ready to accept what God was offering.

22
Oliver

Hey.

        Hey.

Can you meet me tonight after play practice?

        After dinner. 7:30?

Perfect. Preddy Park?

        Ok.

Later that day

While the thermometer had finally inched above freezing, the night air still had a frigid chill to it that stung my face. Maybe meeting outside was a bad idea. *Too late now*—I was halfway to the park. I reluctantly took my hands out of my pockets and tried to zip my black, puffy jacket up even more, but it was already to the top.

The park held a tiny playground about halfway between Darla's and my house. It was a small area, covered in a layer of mulch, with a swing set, climbing wall, and curving slide, all in primary colors. While there was still some snow on the ground, the swing set looked relatively dry, so I took a seat while I waited for Darla. I looked up at the night sky, admiring all of the glowing stars. My thoughts drifted to Julian—it was a few hours earlier where he was, and I wondered what he was up to right now, and if the stars looked the same to him in California as they did here. One thing I was sure of: Christmas had been downright depressing with just Dad and me. It just wasn't the same without my brother. I missed him. A lot.

I didn't have much time to think, as I heard a soft crunch in the snow and glanced back to see Darla approaching. Her hair looked beautiful, cascading in neat waves over her shoulders, under her cream-colored hat. She didn't speak, just smiled, and took a seat on the swing next to mine. She wrapped her gloved hands around the chains and idly rocked back and forth.

"Hi," I started, seeing my breath when I spoke. It nearly disappeared by the time Darla answered.

"Hi." Her voice sounded so soft, almost soundless, like snowflakes falling.

"Thanks for coming out tonight. How was play practice?"

"Good. Charlotte and I had to work together on our duet. It was exhausting, but better than I could have hoped for."

"Good," I replied, not sure what else to say. The silence

between us was growing more awkward by the second, so I decided just to get right to it. "Look, I'm sorry about today—" I started, only to be immediately cut off.

"No, Ollie, I'm sorry." She twisted in the swing to face me. "You're entitled to your own opinion and I should be more understanding." Of course, Darla would take the blame, yet I couldn't help but smile in surprise as I was again reminded of how thoughtful she was.

"I do need to apologize. I got angry about something that had nothing to do with you," I admitted.

"So, tell me what it was about," she said in a matter-of-fact way that made me suspect she already knew.

"I guess I just don't see things the way you do. A lot of people tried to tell me God was with me when my mom died, and I just didn't feel like that did any good—not that I'm trying to say you are wrong for believing. But maybe God just isn't for me . . ." I tried confessing as gently as possible. I didn't want to fight, but I also didn't want to hide how I truly felt. I'd gone to church once with Darla because it was important to her, and it was nice, I guess, but I just felt like an outsider looking in at a party to which I hadn't been invited. And I didn't know if I even *wanted* to be invited to this particular party.

Darla shook her head with a look of pity, and for some reason, that annoyed me. I didn't see how my having a different opinion than hers was a reason for sympathy. I leaned back in the swing, holding the cold chains in my bare hands, and looked back up at the stars as an excuse to avoid eye contact.

"Ollie, I don't want to 'preach' at you, lecture you or pressure you to do or believe anything you don't want to. But I can't let this go without clarifying something about our earlier *discussion.*"

We both knew by the way she emphasized "discussion" that it was nothing of the sort. My Word-of-the-Day calendar suddenly popped into my mind right now, and I remembered the word *euphemism* from a month or two ago.

"Prayer isn't always about helping you fix things or change things. Sometimes it's more about getting you through things," she said with finality, indicating this would be the perfect time for me to tell her I understood, and then move on from this debate. But for some reason, I didn't want to let it go.

"I don't need help getting through things," I told her, my voice coming out a little more defensive than I anticipated.

"You don't *think* you need help."

My eyes immediately darted to hers at this comment. *One point for Darla. And I thought I was the one who was confrontational* . . . Before I could offer a rebuttal, she rushed to explain.

"Ollie, I don't want to fight with you. I came here tonight to apologize and be helpful in any way that I could. Sometimes I forget what you've gone through, and sometimes it's so painfully obvious that I worry about you."

Worry about me? "What is that supposed to mean?" I asked without a hint of anger. I genuinely had no idea what she meant.

"You are wonderful, Ollie. You have everything going your way. You get straight A's, play varsity baseball, you are a talented photographer—all that stuff is great, but you are missing something. I sometimes see sadness in your eyes when you talk about your family, and not just your mom, but your brother and dad, too. Sometimes I see it when you do well on an exam or take an amazing photo—there is this lack of joy, like you can't believe how special you are or won't let yourself be as happy as you could be. I think you're missing the peace that I know you could have if you let God in your life. I think you got so mad today at the idea of prayer because you haven't actually accepted your mom's death and you haven't let God comfort you."

Her comments awoke an anger in me I didn't know I had. Despite the chill in the air, my face felt hot and my chest tightened with the need to explode. I jerked up off the swing and stood in front of her. How could she possibly know any of this? Was she there when my mom died? *No.* Did she know how bad things were compared to how they were now? *No again.* I felt like I was holding so much in and desperately needed to release it and gasp for air.

"I *am* missing something, Darla. Two things, actually—my mother and my brother. I'm sorry that I am not as happy as you would like me to be. Maybe God can bring my mother back from the dead and Julian back home to Virginia?" I practically shouted, asking as if it were a legitimate question. She didn't take the bait and managed to stay calm even while I was revving up the jerk meter. *Why am I being so cruel?*

"No. But He can heal you." She didn't flinch at all from my outpouring of emotion, standing strongly by her beliefs. I admired her for that, and at the same time, I hated her for what she said.

"I don't need to be healed."

"Really?" She paused, as if choosing her words carefully. "I did. I won't ever compare losing a parent to having your parents go through a divorce, but I did feel broken in a completely different way than, I imagine, you do. I felt my dad didn't love me; I felt abandoned. It hurt so much, Ollie. I took it out on my brother and mom, even though *I knew* it wasn't their fault. But God has always seen me through hard times. I remembered, eventually, that I couldn't survive the divorce if I depended on someone else, like my dad, for my happiness. You can only rely on God. True happiness is finding yourself through God's love, not someone else's. I am just trying to help you, Ollie."

I stared at her for a moment or two after her declaration, the night still eerily quiet, allowing me to focus on the sound of her words, now fading away.

"Wow," I stated, a little too emphatically. Darla let out a sigh of relief, misinterpreting this as if I were really considering what she said. I was. But not in the way she thought.

"I never realized how judgmental you are," I said in a biting tone that didn't sound like me. Even before the words left my mouth, I knew I shouldn't have said them. *Then why did I say them?* Yet I still couldn't bring myself to take them back.

"What?" Darla breathed into the air. I saw her eyes misting. A single tear rolled down her cheek. I turned to walk away, but stopped myself. Facing her one more time, I looked pointedly into her eyes.

"I don't want your help, and more to the point, I don't *need* your help." Then, like an angry parent scolding a child, I wagged my finger at her and added, "Keep your theories—and your religion   to yourself." I was on a roll with my selfishness. Not a roll, an avalanche. Why not add one more affront?

"I think we should break up." I ended my tirade and walked away.

23

Julian

A few days later

Christmas was a cold one in California, but not because of the weather. Aunt Sarah's demeanor was almost cold enough to equal the "blizzard of the decade" temperatures back home in Virginia. I owed her tremendously, and I tried to show her how grateful I was for what she had done, but the hurt I'd caused her just couldn't be washed away like footprints in a morning tide.

After she met with the principal at my school, I was fortunate enough to be given a suspension over the holidays, rather than expulsion. She argued that I had nothing to do with the school break-in, and cheating alone, while "reprehensible," shouldn't keep me from being readmitted. She also promised the principal there would be no further skipping class or cheating. Dad got involved, obviously, managing to get my teachers to send weekly grade updates and reports to attest I was attending—and doing well—in class. I never heard so much disappointment in his voice as on the day I had to tell him about the cheating—and that's saying a lot. In the days following my confession, his words, delivered in a tone as somber as a judge issuing a life sentence, kept popping up in my mind: "waste of time," "no future," "failure."

The fight Sarah and my dad had the day of my suspension made me sick to my stomach with guilt. I sat in my room on the edge of the bed, afraid to move or be seen and rock the proverbial boat any further. I could hear a lot of the phone conversation between them, even though she'd stepped outside on the balcony.

"Keith, it's not like I knew what he was up to." *Pause.*
"I know, but I don't think sending him home is the answer." *Another pause.*
"Do *you* even know your own son?" *Aggravated sigh and pause.*
"He is *not* taking advantage of me," *Righteous indignation.*
"I do, *too*, have control of him!" *Short pause.*

"Keith, when was the last time you talked to Julian? I mean really talked to him? I don't think this is just about him not wanting to go to school. He needs you more in his life." *Exasperated sigh.*
"He doesn't have to be *there* for you to show more of an interest!" *Silence.*

The rest of the conversation was either cordial . . . or whispered in harsh tones because I couldn't hear anymore.

Aunt Sarah came inside a couple minutes later, walked past my room, and glanced at me. Then, without a word or a smile, she continued into her room and closed the door gently behind her.

God, what have I done?

I kept all my promises and went back to school—for real this time. When teachers would allow it, I even did extra credit assignments to keep from failing. There was no sign of Liam or Pete, and I was grateful for that. I was not ready to forgive Liam for what he did. First, I found out the janitor was paid $300 for the key to the school office, which means Liam lied to me, and I alone had footed the bill for the answers. Second, when he was caught, he gave up my name. *What the heck?* Friends don't do that.

Things were going well for a couple of weeks, and while I felt like I had broken something between my aunt and me, she still showed me kindness, asking about my day, offering to help with homework, and keeping my favorite Rocky Road ice cream in the house. She loved me, I knew that, but I worried that some part of her regretted ever allowing me to come stay with her.

Unfortunately, I didn't have to wonder for long. Aunt Sarah still had to work the occasional night shift and left me at home to fend for myself for dinner. This usually entailed me walking to the convenience store on the corner and picking up a sandwich or microwavable pizza.

Tonight, I left the condo at around 6 p.m., the sky awash with the purple and orange hues cast by the setting sun. The streets were busy with cars and pedestrians, creating a constant hum of background noise while I walked mindlessly down the sidewalk, watching dusk fade to darkness in a cloudless sky.

It wasn't until I was nearly ten feet away from him that I realized Liam was standing outside of the convenience store, leaning against the glass window and glancing down at his watch impatiently. I recognized his bright yellow "Lakers" hat with the purple rim before I recognized his face. A wave of anger and anticipation at catching him off-guard washed over me, knocking me off balance for a moment. I paused, then crept up silently, giddy as a hunter about to catch his prey. I waited until I was just a foot away, then I practically jumped in his line of sight, standing squarely in front of him. Liam was just a bit shorter than I was, so I bent down so he could see me under his hat, then callously lifted my hand and flicked my fingers under the rim, knocking it off his head.

"Hey, Liam," I greeted snidely, leaning my face into his with an uncomfortable closeness. "How's it going?"

"Julian!" He startled and laughed nervously. He tried to take a step back, but there was no room to move. "Where have you been? I've been trying to call you," he continued with a cold smile. I tilted my head in fake consideration. "That's funny; my number hasn't changed. Let me see your cell phone. I'll check to see if you have the right one," I suggested, my voice dripping with malice. I wasn't going to do anything with his phone, of course—at least I wasn't planning on it. I just wanted to make him nervous. It worked. He made a show of patting the front and back pockets of his jeans with his hands.

"I must have left it at home," he answered with another nervous laugh.

"Huh, imagine that!"

"Listen, about the school thing . . . I wanted to apologize," he beamed, dragging out the word "apologize" as if it were synonymous with "party."

"For what? Taking my money or ratting me out to the principal?"

"Oh, no, no, no, it wasn't like that." He laughed like it

was all a misunderstanding that we could simply write off. "I was supposed to pay the janitor half before, and half after. So, it's a good thing I didn't pay him everything up front, yeah?"

"Not for me. Not if you were expecting my 'half' to be the first installment."

"I was going to pay you back, bro." He sounded almost hurt that I would suspect him of anything. *How did I not see how conniving he was before?*

"And what about giving my name up?" I asked.

"Oh, no, man. I didn't do that. It must have been someone else."

"Pete?"

"Nah, not Pete."

"Who else is there, Liam?" I pressed. "Do you think maybe *I* told someone?" I gripped him by the collar of his hoodie and pushed him hard into the glass window behind him, hearing its slight vibration. "Do you think I'm that stupid?" My voice was rising along with the tension. I should have been worried about drawing a crowd, but the only thing I could think of was how my "friend" had betrayed me. Liam put his hands up in surrender.

"No, man, no. I . . . I don't know what happened," he stuttered, his eyes wide with fear. I'd had about enough of his lies. He was just another example of what was wrong in my life, and I didn't want to see his face in front of me anymore—not ever again. Years of anger that had been steadily brewing rose up from the pit of my stomach, my limbs shaking from the rush of adrenaline. A desperate feeling gripped me that I had to act; if I didn't, I'd explode. I clenched my fist, digging my nails sharply into the palm of my hand. Then, tightening my grip on Liam's hoodie, I drew back my arm. *Crack!*

A sharp pain exploded in my head, like an electric current surging inside my skull. Something had hit me from behind, but before I could process what it was, I was freefalling, too fast to brace myself. My head hit the sidewalk with a sickening *thud*, my skin scraping on the rough concrete.

"Run, man. Run!" I heard faintly. I was lying on my side, watching two sets of sneakers run away from the store, one set definitely Liam's. I lifted myself slowly onto my elbows, but had to stop and wait for the twinkling lights I was seeing to fade before pushing myself all the way up. *Deep breath. Just take a deep breath.*

"Are you ok?" I thought I heard someone say, but it was muffled, like they were talking under water. I couldn't even tell where the voice was coming from. Next thing I knew, two strong hands reached under my armpits and hoisted me up. They held me there until I was steady on my feet. I turned to look into the concerned eyes of an older man with green, hooded eyes. His face was creased in concern.

"Thanks," I mumbled. Then I tried to ease myself off of him to stand up on my own.

"You should go to the hospital, young man. Let me call an ambulance," the man continued, following with an outstretched hand.

"That's ok. I know where it is."

24
Oliver

The same day

Two customers had just left the small dining area in the deli. I wiped down the tables with a damp dishcloth while Hannah rang up another customer at the counter. After the chime of the register, I looked up to see the customer leave and the door close, leaving just Hannah and me after the evening rush. I should have left while I had a chance and gotten back home to work on my science project, but I had more pressing matters on my mind than protons and neutrons.

"Hannah, do you believe in God?" I called from the deserted tables. She spared me a quick glace while counting the till.

"Of course."

"Have you always believed in God?" I pressed. She put the money down, closed the drawer, and gave me her full attention.

"Is this about your mother, Oliver? Because she was a Christian and I have no doubt she is with our Lord and Savior right now, in a better place," she said with a nod of finality, as if her word were the final say-so.

"Ah, no, it's not about Mom. But I didn't know she was a Christian. How did I not know that?" I asked, truly perplexed. We'd never gone to church or grown up hearing stories about Jesus. I thought Grandma Laney gave us a book of Bible stories once when we were little. I could remember its light blue cardboard cover with a picture of a ship and lots of animals, but I couldn't remember actually reading it.

"It isn't for me to say." Hannah shrugged, with a far-off look in her eyes that signaled to me she didn't *know* the answer, rather than didn't want to say. "But what I do know," she continued with another authoritative head nod, "is that your mother sat by my side when my husband was dying of cancer. She held my hands tight and prayed with me all through the night until Peter passed. She spoke to God for me when I couldn't find the strength," Hannah said with a sense of awe in her voice. *Was she proud of my mom? Or maybe just grateful?* I felt a sudden stab of regret that I couldn't talk to my mom about this for myself.

"But how can you know for sure that she believed in God?" I continued.

"I guess you're right, Oliver. I can't know for sure. But I worked alongside your mother for years, was a guest in her home, and she in mine. Observing her life on the outside, she was a woman of good deeds, compassion, strength, and patience. I took this to be her faith shining through. So"—she paused and tilted her head in my direction with mischief in her eyes—"if this isn't about your mother, *who* is it about, *hmmm*?"

"No one, I guess." I avoided making eye contact and wiped the tables down again, even though they didn't need it.

"No one, eh? It's not about that pretty girl that stops by the deli nearly evv–err–ryy day?" She drew out her words in a tease. I couldn't admit to Hannah what a jerk I had been to Darla and how she would probably never speak to me again. I walked back behind the counter, threw my dishcloth in the sink, and grabbed the broom.

"What happened, Oliver?" Hannah's simple question, spoken with such loving concern, almost brought me to tears. Sometimes her words had a way of enveloping you into a hug, when you least expected it. And most needed it.

"We broke up," I stated curtly, and took the broom back toward the dining area.

"Humph," she grunted, "and what does this have to do with God?" I swept under the first table, considering my answer carefully. When I looked up and saw Hannah still waiting patiently, I confessed.

"She said some things, things about me needing God in my life. But my life is fine; I don't need someone telling me to fix problems that aren't there."

"And what problems 'aren't' there?"

"Hannah, do you think of me as a happy person?" I ventured, changing the direction of our conversation so that I didn't have to revisit Darla's comments about what was "missing" in my life.

"Oliver, I have known you since you were in diapers, and I'm so proud of the young man you have become," she said, her eyes glossy with tears. "You are smart, kind-hearted, and talented. But only *you* can know if you are truly happy."

More than anything, I'd wanted her to say, "*Yes, Oliver, you radiate happiness. You are the happiest, most contented person I know.*" Hannah knew me better than Darla, after all, so I trusted her word one hundred percent. Instead, she turned the question squarely back on me. And what scared me the most was that, if I thought about it, I didn't know the answer myself. I started to wonder if Darla's words were true.

25
Sarah

Later that day

"Sarah?" A voice called to me behind the desk at the nurse's station. I looked up from my chart to see Deirdre with a concerned look on her face.

"Yeah?" I answered, hoping it wasn't Mr. Steinhoff, one of my patients who was supposed to have come out of surgery an hour ago.

"I just got a call that your nephew is here," she explained in a gentle voice.

"Julian? Is he in the waiting room?" I asked, confused.

"No, um, he's in room three with Dr. Nguyen."

"Wh–what?" I stuttered, but didn't stick around to get confirmation. I started walking briskly down the hallway, but it quickly turned into a jog as my imagination took hold. *Did the condo catch on fire? Did he break something? Is he too young to leave home alone? What have I done?*

"Julian!" I exclaimed as I pushed open the heavy room door without a knock. Not very professional or considerate, I realized as an afterthought, but neither was the fact that I shoved the kind and eminently qualified Dr. Nguyen out of the way of my nephew.

"What happened?" I asked while examining the scrape on his forehead, careful not to bump his hand, which was holding an ice pack to the back of his head.

"I'm fine, Aunt Sarah," Julian explained in a quiet voice. "I didn't want to trouble anyone. I just asked the receptionist if I could see you, and I was brought in here."

"He hasn't been admitted?" I jerked my head quickly toward Dr. Nguyen. He gave me a sly smile, like a parent would give to a child who'd just unintentionally done something cute. Relieved he'd found the overbearing parenting act endearing rather than offensive, I gathered myself together and smiled at him weakly.

"No, Sarah. He's fine. Just a scrape and a nasty bump," he confirmed.

"No headache? Dizziness? Do you feel sick to your stomach?" I continued anyway.

"I mean, the place where I got hit hurts, and I felt dizzy for like, a second, when I stood up, but then I was fine."

"How did you get here? How did this happen?" Questions swarmed like angry bees in my head.

"I think that's my cue to leave," Dr. Nguyen interjected as he placed a small penlight back in his coat pocket. "Remember to leave that ice in place, Julian," he added on his way out.

"Thank you, Dr. Nguyen, so much—" I rushed to get out

the words before the door closed. Then, I turned my attention on Julian. "What happened?"

"I got in a fight with Liam," he stated, head down, looking up at me through those long lashes of his.

Oh, no! I dropped my head to my hands, obscuring my face, trying not to cry. *This can't be happening.* I slid my hands down, folded as if in prayer, resting my chin against them in thought.

"Aunt Sarah, I didn't mean for this to happen. I didn't go looking for him. I ran into him at the convenience store."

I heard his sincere explanation as the words raced out of his mouth. I was devastated, and not because of this fight, but because of what it meant. Keith was right: I didn't know what I was signing up for when I agreed to have a fifteen-year-old boy come stay with me. Julian was a good kid, really, but he was full of so much anger. Angry at what—his dad, his mom?—I didn't know. But I did know that living with his "cool aunt" in California wasn't going to solve any of his problems.

"I believe you, Julian. Really, I do."

"But?"

"But something has got to change. Not now, but when we get back to the condo, we need to seriously talk about whether California is the right place for you."

"But I'm not skipping school! I wasn't looking to get into a fight!" he pleaded, his voice cracking as tears welled up.

Oh, no. Please don't cry. I don't know if I can handle that.

"I know, Julian. But that doesn't change the fact that these things keep happening."

"So, you don't want me anymore?" He asked, not in disbelief, but with a finality to his voice like he had expected this all along. If it were possible for my heart to break any more, it just had.

"Oh my goodness, I *do* want you. I definitely want you here. You are so awesome, so sweet, so much fun to be around, and I love you very, very much," I quickly explained, desperate for him to believe me. Yet, that didn't prevent what had to come next. "But, Julian, I don't think I am what's best for you."

"So, who is? Dad? Aunt Sarah, he doesn't want me! Please, he might say he'll take me, but trust me, he doesn't want me back." Tears were streaming down his face. Julian dragged his sleeve across his cheeks, trying to wipe them away, but that was as effective as using a cotton ball to wipe the blood from a stab wound.

I threw my arms around him, my face streaked with my own tears, and held him in my arms.

"I love you, Julian. Please know that. I love you, and we will get through this. Together. I promise," I cried, with one hand stroking the back of his hair like I imagined my sister might have done.

"How?" he asked, his voice muffled from my embrace.

"I don't know, Julian. But we will."

WEATHER UPDATE: The Worst is Over

Staff Reporter, PAF NEWS

SUGAR HOLLOW—Power outages and a few storm-related injuries have been reported throughout Sugar Hollow and surrounding areas due to the recent storm, but the snow seems to be finally tapering off.

As many as 7 inches of snow fell across parts of southern Virginia last night. The snow contributed to slick roads and several school districts closing or delaying.

26
Keith

Late January

With Ollie home from school due to the snow, and nearly no one traveling on the icy roads, I decided to do something I hadn't done in nearly fourteen years: I closed the deli for the day. March was right around the corner, and that meant many late-night baseball games and practices for Ollie, leaving us little time together. And while I hadn't made much of an effort over the last three years to make quality time for my family, that was about to change.

Feeling my way through the dimly lit attic, I grabbed a large cardboard box labeled "Books," weighing more than I thought the poorly taped box could handle. Carefully, I stepped down the rickety folding stairs, balancing the box while trying not to step on Harry. *Why that dog insists on always being underfoot is beyond me.* After closing the attic and brushing the dust off the box, I carried it to the living room, Harry on my heels.

The living room was quiet, the soft browns and blues of the décor adding to its calming effect. Anna, of course, was the one who did the decorating. She'd chosen the color scheme, painstakingly poring over all the options before making her decisions. At the time I hadn't paid much attention—decorating was never my thing—but now I could appreciate how the colors complemented each other, much like Anna and I complemented each other. Her *punctilious* nature (one of her favorite words), combined with my easygoing attitude, had always created a great balance in our marriage, and in our parenting. It had taken me too long to realize that I needed to somehow restore that balance with my family, even though she was gone.

Placing the box on our small coffee table, I could almost picture Anna cringing at the sight of the dirty cardboard on the rustic, chestnut furniture she'd picked out. I moved it on the floor, as if appeasing her, and ripped it open. Finding over a dozen books of Anna's, ranging in topics from music theory, to good parenting, to cooking techniques, I took them out, one-by-one, fanning them cover to cover, and letting the dust fly off.

"What are you doing?" Ollie asked as he walked into the room carrying his bowl of cereal, wearing an old pair of sweatpants and a high school baseball sweatshirt. That boy was always eating. It was 9:30 a.m. and I was pretty sure this was his second breakfast.

"I'm getting out some of your mother's things from the attic. I was looking for something. Thought I'd go ahead and put these back on the bookshelf. What do you think?" Ollie gave a noncommittal shrug. I'm sure the books on parenting weren't appealing—at least, *they better not be*—but who knew when we'd want to glance at the others, even if it was just to remember that Anna had held it at some point. I was a little disappointed at Ollie's indifference, having clung to the futile hope that putting his mom's books back out would somehow magically fill the gaping hole her absence had left.

"Ollie, I want to talk to you."

"Ok," he mumbled, trying not to dribble milk out of his mouth while answering.

How many times do I have to tell the boys not to talk with food in their mouth? I resisted the urge to shake my head in disapproval. He took a seat in the armchair while I sat on the couch, books still in hand.

"Did I ever tell you about how I helped your mom plan our wedding?"

"No," he answered with a shrug, his attention fixed on his bowl of Cheerios. It was not often I talked about Anna, and Ollie probably wasn't sure what to expect.

"Well, that is probably because I only caused more problems rather than actually helping," I admitted. "Your mom wanted the perfect fairytale wedding—not expensive or extravagant," I quickly clarified, not wanting to give him the wrong idea about his mother. "She just wanted everything to be really beautiful. She loved the idea of a backyard reception, but it had to look just right. She got these huge white tents for her mother's yard where we put tables underneath to eat—"

"I think I saw pictures," Ollie interjected with a nod. We'd had a few pictures framed from the ceremony, but pictures from the reception were stored in an album somewhere, probably collecting as much dust as the books in hand. But I wasn't surprised that Anna would have taken the time to show the boys the album. She loved sitting with them, sharing stories and making new memories.

"Yeah?" I continued. "Did you see she had this material, I don't know what it was—it probably has some fancy name—but it was this sheer white fabric draped from ceiling to floor all around the tent?" I paused to give Ollie time to answer, and he obliged with a nod.

"Every detail was important to her. It was stunning. Like she was." My thoughts drifted away from my original purpose as I took a minute to remember the twinkling strands of lights she had my dad and father-in-law hang up the night before around the perimeter of the tent. I remembered vases of red calla lilies on each table. And, of course, I remembered exactly how she looked in her white lace gown.

"Anyway, your mom was a perfectionist and insisted on doing everything herself, but I felt bad for all the work she was doing, so I offered to help. She gave me one job. 'Keith,' she said, 'I interviewed a bunch of photographers. I know the one I want, but I have to give him a deposit immediately. Can you drop off a check?' she asked. 'Of course,' I answered," then narrowed my gaze at Ollie. "Back then," I reminded him, "we couldn't pay instantly over the computer.

"That morning, your Uncle Jack called me. He'd gotten a new jon boat and asked if I wanted to go fishing. I was off from work, it was a beautiful day, and I always had a hard time saying no to fishing. So he came over, we picked up some nightcrawlers for the fish, packed a couple of sandwiches, and went out on the lake for a few hours.

"We were having the best time, enjoying the quiet and

catching a few crappie and perch. It was late afternoon when your uncle caught a beautiful six-pound bass—although he'll swear to this day that it was at least eight. I took a picture with my cell phone thinking I would show your mom. She wasn't all that interested in fishing, but she humored me by listening to my stories anyway. Just minutes after I took that picture, she called. I picked up the phone cheerfully when she asked me in an *I-mean-business* voice, 'Keith, where are you?' I was still in a good mood and gushed about my brother's big catch. But as soon as the words left my mouth, I remembered I was supposed to go to see the photographer that day."

"What did you say?" Ollie asked, his spoon suspended in mid-bite.

"Well, I was kind of shocked and I think I just mumbled out an *oh no* or something like that."

"What did *she* say?" he questioned with more curiosity.

"Well, that's the funny part of the story. She starting yelling, and even Uncle Jack heard her yell through the phone: 'You had one job!' But that's about all she got out before the high-pitch volume of her yelling startled me into dropping the phone. Right. Into. The lake."

"Oh, no," Ollie started with a mixture of disbelieve and laughter. "Did you get in trouble when you saw her afterwards? I bet she was so mad . . ." His questions spilled out, and he'd even put his half-finished bowl of cereal down.

"Oh, yeah, big time. First, I got yelled at. Then, I got the silent treatment. But it all worked out in the end. I took care of it the next day and your mom, obviously, forgave me."

"Yeah, but I bet she didn't ask for your help again, did she?"

"No, she did not," I answered with a wistful smile. Sometimes even looking back on a fight with Anna was just as nostalgic as looking back at one of those so-called more perfect memories. I missed not only her smile, her laughter, and her kindness, but also her stubbornness, compulsiveness, and even the fleeting moments of hostility. "But there is a reason I was reminded of all this today." I took a deep breath, letting the memory wash over me like an unexpected cool breeze.

"I was chewed out by your Aunt Sarah this week. Boy, she got it honest, I tell you. Both of those sisters know how to put you in your place. Kinda made me miss your mom," I added with complete sincerity.

"What?" Ollie drew out the word in disbelief, but the smile on his face let me know he was dying to hear the whole story.

"It's true. Aunt Sarah yelled at me about Julian, and about how he's feeling. And more to the point, how I was oblivious to it. She can be scary sometimes." I added the last thought in a near whisper, thinking about how she could give my drill sergeant back in the Air Force a run for his money. "Oh, and I got yelled at by Hannah too this week," I reported.

"Hannah?" Ollie pressed. "What did she yell at you for?" He'd picked up his cereal again and was shoveling in the rest of the Cheerios with rapt attention.

"She told me, 'Keith. Enough is enough. You get those boys to church, or I'll fix you with a switch,'" I reiterated in my best imitation of Hanna's voice.

"No . . . she didn't," Ollie laughed. I loved seeing him smile. I didn't see it much.

"Well, maybe not the part about the switch. But it was

implied." We were both laughing now at the thought of it.

"Ollie, things are going to change around here," I added with what I hoped was enough conviction to confirm my commitment.

"This is so weird," Ollie continued the conversation, placing his now empty bowl on the table in front of him. "We've been a family that has never gone to church, and all of a sudden God is the only thing we're talking about."

"That's not entirely true. Your mother went to church when we were dating—even convinced me to go a few times," I added, with raised eyebrows. *Yeah, I know what it's like to want to make your girlfriend happy by going to church.* "But," I continued, "when I came back from the war, I just kept making excuses for not wanting to go. I guess I wasn't sure what to believe in anymore. Your mother kept going on her own though—even took you boys when you were young. But as you got older, and our responsibilities increased, plus the fact I was never helpful in this regard, she gradually stopped. I should have made more of an effort."

"So, you believe in God?" Ollie asked bluntly, taking me by surprise. This was entirely new territory in terms of father–son conversation, and for a moment I panicked, wondering how I was supposed to respond.

"Honestly? I don't know. But I'm not going to let my questions stop you and your brother from getting your own answers. Your mother would have loved the idea of me taking you both to church every Sunday. In fact, lately, I can just feel her looking down at us, yelling, and using the opportunity to test out new vocabulary words: 'What are your doing, Keith? Stop with the *despondency* and start being a *stellar* father,'" I added another imitation.

"You are a stellar father," Ollie added quickly and forcefully, as if this made it fact. Happy as I was to hear the love in his voice, I didn't feel, at that moment, that I deserved it.

"Thank you, Ollie. But I want to be a better one. And I will be. We are going to be a family again, and that means talking more about things, whether it's about my past, or about your mom, school, or even God. And I promise, Ollie, to be a better listener, too."

Local Animal Shelter Asking for the *Ulti-MUTT* Help

Staff Reporter, PAF NEWS

SUGAR HOLLOW—In the wake of the recent winter storm, the Sugar Hollow Animal Shelter is accepting dozens of animals in need of foster care and/or adoption from neighboring counties. The shelter will receive several kittens, cats, dogs, and puppies this week in an effort to help overcrowded shelters in other areas. The shelter is asking for volunteers to give their time or a financial donation to support this endeavor. Please contact the shelter if you are able to help.

27
Oliver

February

I was wrong when I told Darla I was missing two things in my life—I should have realized that I was missing at least one more—my dad. I didn't know how much I missed him until we'd sat down to talk—I mean really talk—the other day. For the first time in a long time, I was happy.

I was grateful Darla cared enough to challenge me to think about whether I was truly happy. I was grateful that Hannah confronted my dad. I was grateful Aunt Sarah cared enough to try to fix things. And I was grateful Dad had listened. Was this all God at work? The thought never would have entered my mind in the past. *But now?*

I knew one thing for certain: I needed to apologize to Darla. Big time. According to the store's webpage, Pet Palace was open, which seemed strange in this weather. I decided to take the risk and go, knowing that if it were open, she would be there.

By the time I'd showered, found some clean clothes in my room, and walked to Pet Palace, it was past noon. Much to my surprise, when I went in, I saw at least a dozen customers. I'd never seen that many people at the pet shop before—maybe one or two customers, three at the most. But today it was like Black Friday before Christmas.

I spotted Darla walking briskly down the aisle with a customer at her heels.

"Hey!" I mouthed, giving her a small, hesitant wave. She did a double take when she saw me. Maybe I imagined it, but I thought she looked happy to see me, at least for a fleeting moment. Very fleeting. Maybe it was just wishful thinking. Her eyes narrowed and her chin rose as she walked past me. *Ouch.* Maybe showing up unannounced at her place of work was a bad idea. But I couldn't wait a second longer to apologize.

I pretended to look at some beta fish while I waited for her to finish with her current customer. As soon as she was done, I rushed to her side before someone else got to her first.

"Can you help me find some treats for my dog, Harry?" I asked, pretending like I was just another stranger in the store. "He is really particular in his old age. He gets really bad gas," I whispered, as if wanting to shield my dog, who wasn't even there, from embarrassment. "I could really use an expert opinion." Darla's head tilt and a look of annoyance confirmed this wasn't going to be easy.

"I can't talk right now, Ollie. In case you haven't noticed, we're a little busy today," she said with more attitude than I knew she was capable of. *Note to self: never underestimate*

Darla.

"Yeah, why is that?" I asked sincerely, watching the busy shoppers filling their carts with supplies. Darla hesitated, perhaps deciding whether she was going to give me an answer or not. I guess my charm won her over. *Yeah, probably not.*

"It's because of the storm. The local shelter has taken in all the strays it can handle. We volunteered to help out, so we have a bunch of kittens in the back, as well as a few cats, all needing homes. The place has been crazy all morning."

"That's great, right? That means people are buying the animals?"

"Not really. We are getting a lot of people willing to foster the kittens, which means their home is only temporary. What we need are more people to adopt them—especially the older ones. Everyone wants the kittens."

"That's sad, but I guess it makes sense," I thought, remembering when we got Harry. We wouldn't settle for anything but a puppy at the time.

"Yeah, I just wish more people understood how adorable and loving these animals are. I just know they would be adopted if people could actually see them." She frowned, her shoulders slumped in defeat, until a customer's familiar cry of, "*Excuse me?*" jolted her out of her thoughts. Before she turned to help them, I reached for her arm.

"When can I talk to you, Darla? I really, really want to apologize. I'm a jerk, I know, and you don't have to forgive me, I don't expect you to. But please just let me apologize," I practically begged. Who was I kidding? I *was* begging.

"I gotta go," she murmured as she wriggled out of my grasp. But then, perhaps as an afterthought, she turned back.

"I finish work at six, but I have to stay until seven." *Perfect,* I silently cheered.

Just out of curiosity, I headed to the back to have a look at the new "inventory." I'd always thought of myself as more of a dog person, but I had to admit . . . those kittens were cute. I slowly strayed over to the adult cats, taking a look at them as well. There was a giant orange fur ball named Hagrid. I smiled knowingly; Darla must have helped name the strays in the shop. Hagrid put one paw up on the metal bars of his cage, and with a soft meow, pawed at me with the other. I put my finger out to pet the limb while he tried to play.

And that is when the idea hit me.

#

I hurried home to collect the supplies I would need: my camera, *obviously,* my small tripod, and my external flash. Now, for props . . . I looked around my room and threw some things in my backpack: my baseball glove, ball, and a black throw blanket. In the bathroom, I dumped some towels out of a decorative wicker basket that Mom had always liked (I'd clean those up later), and then headed to the garage. Dad had a ball of twine and . . . what else? Oh, an old boot. *Yup, that should do it.*

I headed back to the pet shop after I'd eaten spaghetti with Dad, enjoying this new, approachable side of him. By the time I got there, I had about ten minutes before the store was due to close. It looked like Darla was ringing up the last customer, and Mrs. Scott, the owner, was in the back with a mop, starting evening cleanup. I went to talk to her first.

"Hi, Mrs. Scott."

"Hi, Oliver. Is your dad ok? I saw the deli was closed," she asked, pausing her mopping to look me in the eye.

"He's fine. He just decided to take the day off."

"Good for him," she said with gusto, as if coming from someone who knew how hard it was to take a break.

"Mrs. Scott, I wanted to talk to you about something . . ." She eyed my large camera bag and book bag and then answered with an encouraging nod.

"I was thinking about all of the animals you have now, needing adoption. And I thought I could help. I thought I could take pictures of them and we could post them on social media and different websites. I've gotten pretty good at photography, and I think I could really get some good shots that might make people want to come in and adopt." There was a short pause as she considered my proposal, and I was surprised how nervous I was that she might say "No." I really wanted to do this.

"Hmm . . . Yes, I've seen your photos in the deli. I love the one you have of Hannah, but don't tell her I told you that." She added the last part with a mildly threatening look and a smile. No one wanted to get on Hannah's bad side.

"When were you thinking about doing this?" she asked. I held up my hands, loaded with my equipment.

"How about now?"

An hour later and we were through. I had closeups of kittens sitting inside my mitt, two kittens inside my dad's boot, and another shot with four kittens snuggled in a basket. I had ac-tion shots with the cats playing with the twine and sleepy shots of one older cat playing hide-and-seek in my blanket. Darla and Mrs. Scott helped; my two favorite shots included them. One was with the large orange cat draped over Darla's shoulder, so content to be held, with Darla looking at him adoringly. The other one was of Mrs. Scott holding a small grey and black kitten in front of her, their noses touching.

I waited outside the shop for Mrs. Scott and Darla to finish up inside, hoping Darla would let me walk her home. The sun had dipped far below the horizon, and I rubbed my hands together to keep warm. As I paced nervously up and down the walkway, Darla finally came out, issuing a "Good night," to her boss over her shoulder.

"Can I walk you home?" I blurted out hopefully before she'd even had a chance to take a step.

"Sure." I couldn't quite decipher how she felt by her tone, but I took it as a small victory—and a major relief—that she said "Yes."

As we set out together, carefully navigating the snowy walkway, I took a deep breath and began, "Darla, I'm so sorry. I was a complete jerk. I was wrong to talk to you that way, and I was even wrong about what I was saying." This earned me a surprised sideways glance.

"What do you mean you were *wrong* about what you were saying?"

"I don't know about God. I'm willing to listen, but that's not really the part I meant. You were right about how I'm feeling. With Julian gone, and my dad being so distant all the time, I just kind of accepted the state of being ok   not miserable, but not actually happy either. But something changed. And I want to tell you all about it. In fact, you were the first person I wanted to talk to after things started to shift. But I needed to apologize first."

Darla turned on her heels to face me, the ice beneath her

feet causing her to lose her balance. She slipped slightly and started to sway backwards, her arms reaching out toward me. I grabbed both her arms to steady her, but the step I took in her direction landed me on my own patch of ice. *Oh, no.*

In a very awkward flailing movement, my arms and feet betrayed me. I tried to keep us both upright, but Darla landed on her back in a pile of snow, her hair sprawled out around her, while I face planted next to her, managing to get a mouthful of cold, wet slush.

I rolled over on my back, arms away from her, spitting out the snow.

"Are you ok?" I asked, turning my head toward her, my ear numbly pressed into the white mess. Darla's response started as a giggle; then, a wicked grin spread across her face. Before I knew what had hit me, Darla grabbed a handful of snow and smooshed it into my face. Her giggle quickly turned into a fit of hilarity while she watched me struggle to stand up, intent retaliation. But instead of grabbing a snowball of my own, I just fell back down on my patch of ice.

As we lay side-by-side, breathless with laughter, I reached my arm out between us, fingers extended. She understood my nonverbal request and placed her hand in mine. I squeezed my hand shut, afraid to let her go.

"I'm sorry, Darla," I said again.

"I know," she smiled, then shrugged like it was no big deal. "I forgive you."

28
Julian

Hey Ollie

Who's this?

Ha ha. Sorry I haven't been
around much.

That's what Mom would call a
minimization.

I hate your calendar.

You're just invidious.

I'm coming home in a few

weeks.

I'm glad. Things have been
bad without you here.

You mean worse than
usual?

I think things are going to be
different when you get home. I
mean different from before
you left.

Yeah?

Yeah. Dad actually went
to the batting cages with me
yesterday AND let me teach
him some things I learned in
my photography class.

That's cool. But I'm not sure he
is going to be that happy to see
me. Not after everything.

Don't be fatuous.

You're impossible. . .
Pet Harry for me.

29
Darla

A few days later

On my way to chorus class, I meandered through the hallway, thoughts of my recent science class already fading into a distant memory. Instead of pondering the various phases of mitosis, images of Ollie playing with scruffy old cats filled my mind. I smiled at the mental picture of him dangling his dad's old bootlaces in front of a particularly feisty cat who jumped up unexpectedly, startling Ollie. *I hope he didn't want those laces back . . .*

After Ollie had patiently photographed each of the shelter animals, he posted all his pictures online and immediately got dozens of views. Those turned into over a hundred shares and retweets, which finally led to a record number of adoptions. It was amazing . . . and it got me thinking. How could I help make a difference, too? Lost in concentration, I walked right into something, hard.

Oh, no. It wasn't a *something*, but a *someone*. It was Ada, who was standing outside of the chorus classroom with what looked like a large iced coffee. Ada immediately put her hands out to stop herself from falling and ended up bracing herself against Charlotte with one hand—and the drink in her other spilled out all over the floor and onto Charlotte's shoes. A puddle of creamy brown liquid pooled around her feet.

"You stupid klutz!" Charlotte yelled in a shrill voice that made everyone in the vicinity stop and stare. I wasn't sure if it was directed at Ada or me. Regardless, I was becoming immune to Charlotte's temper tantrums, so I wasn't really fazed by her anger or the gathering crowd.

"Do you know how much these shoes *cost*?" she continued to whine—loudly—while looking down and examining the cutest pair of black ballet flats I had ever seen. They were embroidered with little red flowers and adorned with what looked like a red satin strap. I had little doubt they were expensive. I took a deep breath in preparation for what had to be done.

"I'm sorry, Charlotte. It was my fault," I spoke up, hating to admit it. It wasn't that I minded apologizing when I was guilty of something; it was just, in Charlotte's case, nothing good ever seemed to come from doing the right thing.

"Whatever," she said with an eye roll. "It's not like I don't have at least a dozen pairs of shoes at home," she sneered, eyeing my sneakers with a grin. *Huh?* I felt she'd let me off the hook pretty easily, to be honest. I'd expected another Oscar-winning performance from the poor, victimized damsel in distress. Maybe I was growing on her now that we were in the musical together? *Yeah right.*

For whatever reason, Ada still felt the need to grovel, so she apologized profusely while dabbing at Charlotte's shoes with some paper towels she'd taken from the girls bathroom. No surprise, Charlotte wasn't the least bit appreciative and just pushed Ada away. After the fiasco, everyone went into class and got settled, standing in their assigned spots on the chorus risers. That was when the idea hit me.

"Mrs. Kowalski?" I called out.

"Yes, Darla?" responded our ever-patient chorus teacher, a trait she seemed to have mastered due to her experience and age. She stood in front of the risers, eyes wide with anticipation behind her tortoiseshell glasses, as she gingerly pulled her heavy, crocheted sweater jacket tightly around her flowered dress.

"I have an idea," I called out, still trying to formulate the whole thing in my head.

"Oh. Ok, Darla."

"You know how that family in Preddy Creek lost their home because of the storm?" I asked.

"Yeah, I heard about that!" Florence Reddy called out from the alto section. "The roof collapsed and they had so much water and structural damage that they lost, like, everything they had." A bunch of students turned to each other with nods, sharing accounts of their own version of the story.

"I was thinking," I interjected above the noise, "maybe the chorus club could have a clothing drive? Or some kind of collection for them? They have three children, so I'm sure they need a lot of things."

"That's a great idea, Darla," Mrs. Kowalski said without hesitation, clasping her hands in front of her with genuine enthusiasm. Before she could comment further, another student jumped in.

"Oh! My mom always keeps stuff in the house to have a garage sale someday, but I doubt it will ever happen. I bet she would donate stuff. We have tons of dishes and things," Jill Trencher added.

"And my little brother has so many toys and games. I bet I could take a bunch and he wouldn't even notice," smirked Scott Lewis.

"Well, let's not take things without permission," Mrs. Kowalski interjected. "But do talk to your parents, and I will gladly reach out to the family about dropping things off."

I was excited about the buzz of enthusiasm around me as people considered how they could contribute. It was inspiring. I felt giddy, and I couldn't keep the smile off my face. While the chatter continued, I noticed Ada turn to Charlotte with narrowed eyes and a conspiratorial grin.

"You can donate some of those shoes you have, Charlotte. You have *dozens*, right?" she added loud enough for the entire class to hear. I'm not sure what exactly she hoped to accomplish. If she wanted to expose Charlotte for being selfish, I didn't think there was a single person in the class (maybe the school) who didn't know it already. But if nothing else, it was clear that Ada was fed up being Charlotte's minion and was using this as an opportunity to break ranks.

Without any hesitation, *or thought*, Charlotte showed the extent of her self-centeredness. "No way. I'm not giving up my stuff. What if a tree falls on *my* house? I'll ask my parents to write a check."

Ada didn't push it, and I certainly had no reason to, either. I knew a lost cause when I saw one . . . Much as I disliked

Charlotte, however, I didn't write her off totally. Everyone had some good in them, right? And who knows? Maybe one day she would surprise us all with her selfless generosity and goodwill. It just wasn't going to be that day.

30
Oliver

March

As the bone-chilling temperatures of winter finally gave way to the mild, sunny days of spring, I said a silent cheer of thanks. I welcomed the change in weather and also the opportunity to watch Darla perform in the Spring Musical. I knew she'd be great, of course, but I couldn't have imagined just *how* great. She carried the show, the audience captivated by her voice. Per Hannah's suggestions, I'd brought Darla a bouquet of flowers to present to her at the end, and I wasn't alone. Her brother (with help from her mom, I'm sure) and Harlow also came prepared with their own colorful arrangements. I went to two of the three performances, first with some friends and then with my dad. Even *he* was impressed and gushed to Darla's mom about how proud she must be of her daughter.

And while spring brought with it pink dogwood blossoms, less rain, and the start of baseball, I knew it was just a matter of days before it brought Julian home as well. That is what I was most excited about.

Today was the day our team was going to play against our toughest rival, Western Hollow High. It was about thirty minutes before game time, and parents and friends were already filling the bleachers, staking out their spots with their foldable chairs and, for some of our more vocal critics, leaning against the chain-link fence to get even closer to the action.

Since it was a home game, our team took the field first; I was the starting pitcher. I threw a few practice pitches to our catcher, David Nokes, trying not to get distracted by the crowd. Darla was in the stands with her mom and brother; my dad was supposed to be there, too, but I couldn't see him anywhere.

"Batter up!" a voice boomed. I turned to see the umpire get in position behind home plate. We'd only had a few games so far that season, and we had more wins than losses, but this one meant more than all the others; this one I *really* wanted to win. The opposing team had a reputation for being bad winners, taunting and jeering at the losing team. Last year, they'd lost a home game to us and sulked miserably in their respective dugout, but on the away game they beat us by four runs. As if forgetting that we'd won against them previously, they snickered at us as we slapped hands afterwards, adding comments like "That was a cinch," "Are you gonna make it harder to beat you next time?" "My sister's team coulda beat you guys . . ."

The first batter approached the plate, taking a few practice swings on the way. He got in position, tapping his bat on the plate to measure, then squared up to bat.

I pitched him a fastball, right down the middle.

"Strike!" The umpire shouted, making it sound more like a three-syllable word. *Stee-eer-ike.* The crowd sitting in the home-team section cheered loudly and clapped. David stood and threw the ball back to me, and I readied myself for the next pitch—another fastball.

"Strike two!" the umpire yelled, this time after the batter swung and missed. More cheers erupted from the crowd. Not wanting to fix what wasn't broken, I threw my fastball a third time. *Ping.* The familiar sound of the leather ball hitting a metal bat filled the playing field—a beautiful line drive past our second basemen. The right fielder got the ball and threw it hard to the first baseman, but not before the runner made it there: "Safe!"

I scanned the crowd and still couldn't see my dad, but I could hear my teammates and coach shouting in support. "Alright, that's alright, shake it off. You got this."

Before I pitched to the second batter, David signaled that the guy on first looked like he might try to steal. Just as we'd practiced, I turned and whipped the ball to the first baseman, but the runner got back in time.

Readying myself again, I threw the ball over the plate. Swing and a miss—strike one. Worried that he'd get a hit off, I decided to throw my change-up. It worked. He swung too soon and missed. Strike two. Now it was back to my fastball. I stole a glance at the bleachers. No dad. I threw the ball a third time. *Ping.* A high fly to our shortstop. He caught it, leaving a runner on first with one out.

The third batter stepped up, as cocky a player as I'd ever seen, his jaw opening and closing in an exaggerated motion as he chewed an enormous wad of gum. As he squared up to the plate he winked at me condescendingly, his team cheering him on: "He's got nothing. Hit it hard, Ryan!"

I started with my fastball; it was low and the umpire shouted, "Ball one!" *Damn.*

"Come on, Ollie, you got this!" I heard Darla's little brother shouting, which for some reason released some of the tension and made me smile. I threw again. He hit it straight up, almost.

"Foul ball," the umpire yelled, as David threw his mask off to get to the ball before the guy on first had a chance to steal. Fortunately, he stayed put.

I concentrated, waving off David's signal for a curve ball. It was my least consistent pitch, and I didn't want to use it on someone at the top of the order. So, fastball it was.

Ping. The ball headed right to me on the pitcher's mound. I caught it on the bounce, threw it directly to the second baseman, who sent it to the first baseman: double play. The crowd cheered. The inning was over.

"Way to go, Ollie!" a familiar voice rang out, as we all ran to the dugout for our turn at bat. I knew that voice. I had missed that voice. I turned to see Dad and Julian, leaning against the fence. *What? He's not supposed to be home yet.*

I hesitated for a second, but then quickly recovered. Tossing my glove into the dugout, I ran over to my brother and threw my arms around him in a hug, the noise of the game completely tuned out. He returned the hug, gripping the back of my uniform. Finally, my family was back together.

31
Julian

A few moments earlier

I could see Ollie scan the bleachers a few times looking for Dad, his eyes overlooking us by the fence. I watched, getting caught up in the game, shouting with the crowd and proud of my brother. I didn't realize how much I missed him until that moment. Dad's idea of surprising him was definitely awesome. He'd arranged to pick me up from the airport with Aunt Sarah, who had taken a few days off work to visit with the family.

The tension I first felt at seeing my dad at the baggage claim made my stomach churn. As I hesitantly walked toward him, preparing myself for the familiar look of disappointment in his eyes, I repeated over and over in my head, *It's ok, it will be fine*. When I stood directly in front of him, I felt the need to fill the silence with telling him how sorry I was, begging for forgiveness. But Dad's expression was one more of curiosity than displeasure, as if he were looking me over to make sure I was the same child who left months ago. Before I could begin my pleading about how stupid I'd been, and how I didn't deserve to come home again, he grabbed me in a hug and held me so tight he threatened to break a rib . . . or two. It was totally unexpected—and just what I needed.

Still locked in our hug, my father finally spoke after what felt like minutes. "You're never leaving home again," he whispered in my ear. I was pretty sure it was said out of love, and not meant as a punishment, as he followed up with, "I missed you more than you can possibly imagine." It was like a giant boulder had been lifted from my chest and I could breathe for the first time. Aunt Sarah stood back, letting us have our privacy, and I was thankful. I think she'd seen me cry enough for one lifetime.

After settling in at home for a few minutes and giving Harry some belly rubs and ear scratches, we headed straight to Ollie's game to surprise him. But that wasn't the only surprise of the day. While we stood outside together watching the game, my dad put his hand on my shoulder and turned to partially face me.

"Julian, I want to give you something."

"Ok," I said, a little hesitantly. We were at baseball game. What could he have in mind?

"I've been thinking about this a lot. You are able to get your learner's permit now. I'm not sure what the consequences are yet from your . . . *activities* in California. I can't just let you off without any punishment, but I've decided I'm not taking this away from you. In fact, learning to drive—responsibly—can really help you contribute to family life."

"Ok," I said a second time, just as confused as the first.

Where was this going? And, of course, I knew I would be in some kind of trouble for my *activities*, but honestly, I didn't care what it was. The fact that my dad forgave me and wanted me home was all I needed. I would graciously accept any punishment he gave me.

"So, I've been thinking, and I want to give you Mom's car."

"*Um, huh?* I'm sorry, what?" I'm sure my eyes had widened to saucer size as I tried to process his words.

"You heard me. I want you to have it. I've seen how carefully you've been working on it, and I know your mom would want you to have it, too."

I was shocked, and for some reason, a little embarrassed.

"But, Dad. After everything? I certainly didn't *earn* it." And that, I knew, was why I felt so undeserving.

"No, you did not. But this is not something for you to earn, Julian; it's something I just want you to receive. It's my gift to you. I want you to know how much I love you and how grateful I am to have you home. Also, from now on, I want to spend more time with you. We can work on the car together if you'll let me. How does that sound?"

It was weird to see a look of nervousness in my dad's expression. After all, this guy had fought in a war, seen action in combat zones, and to me he was almost invincible. Something had definitely happened when I was away. Clearly, I wasn't the only one who had turned a corner. In the past, I thought I didn't *want* to spend time with my dad. But that was because I was angry about a lot of things—how he shut down after Mom died, how he stopped showing an interest in Ollie and me. But now? I could physically see the change in him, even as he talked, his attention fully fixed on me. And I knew I was tired of pushing everyone away as well. I knew being a family again was exactly what I wanted—and what we all needed.

"Dad, thank you. That sounds perfect."

Ping. The batter hit a ground ball to Ollie. Ollie threw it to the second baseman and, boom, just like that, double play! We cheered and the inning was over. *Oh, yeah!*

I could see the moment of recognition in my twin's eyes when he picked out my voice in the crowd, the joy in his eyes mirroring my own. He ran over to me and grabbed me in a hug. I hugged him back.

32
Oliver

Later that day

After winning the game five to one, most of the team went to get ice cream at the local Dairy Creamery to celebrate, but I had a celebration of my own I wanted to get to. Dad had invited Hannah and Darla's family over for a barbeque, and of course, Aunt Sarah and Julian were there too.

We sat around in the backyard at a picnic table that hadn't yet seen any use so far this year. Now it was covered with a vinyl, blue and white-checkered tablecloth that I had a feeling Aunt Sarah had picked up when she got the party supplies. Dad made hamburgers and hot dogs, Darla's mom made a chocolate cake with a rich buttercream frosting, and Hannah made a special dish she called potato pudding (which, by the way, she never made for the deli)—it was like a fried potato pancake with bacon and sour cream. We sat around talking, laughing, and just enjoying each other's company. Harry entertained us with his pathetic attempts to get attention—and a stray hotdog—resting his head on everyone's laps, one at a time.

Julian and I didn't have much of a chance to catch up that day, but I wasn't worried. We had plenty of time now that he was back. He did get me alone in the kitchen at one point and told me about the car, with a bit of nervousness, almost like he was asking for my permission.

"Dad already told me; don't worry about it. I'm glad he's giving it to you," I told him, and meant it.

Later in the afternoon, while people were getting seconds and thirds on food, Darla and I took Harry for a walk down the street. I took the opportunity when we were alone to tell her about my mom's car.

"Are you upset?" Darla asked while turning to face me, but my eyes were on Harry for the moment, as he was pulling on his leash and trying to catch a squirrel.

"Nah," I finally answered when I got the mutt under control.

"Your dad just gave Julian your mom's car. I don't know much about it, but that seems like a big deal. Right?"

"Hmm, well . . . yeah. But I'm not upset about it."

"You're a better person than I am. I would totally be jealous," she said, but I didn't believe that for a second. She was just too kindhearted. Besides, I had been jealous at first. And angry, too.

"I guess what I should have said is that I'm not jealous *anymore*. My mom used to have this saying that I thought was really stupid. She'd say, 'As a family, we lift each other up. We are a team.' Julian and I would sometimes try to hoist each other up on top of each other's shoulders, 'lifting' each other up, laughing like crazy. 'Stop causing a ruckus,' she'd yell, or 'If you're going to horse around, go outside.' She was always agitated we didn't take it seriously. But I think that's because I didn't understand. Until now."

"Meaning you can put your own feelings aside and accept just being happy for Julian?" she asked with a nod of understanding.

"Yeah, pretty much. I have a great life—Julian's back, I have a good relationship with my dad now . . . and you," I added, with a smile in her direction. "That's all I could possibly want. I never wanted the car anyway, so why should I compare what I have to what my brother has? I'm happy that Julian is back and can get back on track to find his own happiness. That's all I need."

"You're a pretty amazing guy, Oliver," Darla said while grabbing my free hand, holding it in hers as we walked down the block. After a minute, I stopped and turned to her. She looked at me curiously, holding my stare. I pulled her toward me, until our faces were only inches apart. Then, at the same time, we both leaned in, our lips touching.

We drew apart after the kiss, and I said, "No, you're the amazing one, Darla." She smiled shyly, her face flushed.

As we walked back in a comfortable silence, I marveled at how fortunate I was to have her in my life. Who was I to judge her beliefs? Maybe she had been right all along—about everything—and Hannah, too. Maybe the next chapter in my life wouldn't be *my* plan at all. Maybe it would be . . . *Someone else's*.

Study Guide

The Parable of the Two Sons ~ depicted in Chapter 1
Matthew 21:28-32 (ESV)

"What do you think? A man had two sons. And he went to the first and said, 'Son, go and work in the vineyard today.' And he answered, 'I will not,' but afterward he changed his mind and went. And he went to the other son and said the same. And he answered, 'I go, sir,' but did not go. Which of the two did the will of his father?" They said, "The first." Jesus said to them, "Truly, I say to you, the tax collectors and the prostitutes go into the kingdom of God before you. For John came to you in the way of righteousness, and you did not believe him, but the tax collectors and the prostitutes believed him. And even when you saw it, you did not afterward change your minds and believe him."

Have you ever heard the saying, "actions speak louder than words"? Well, that is essentially what Jesus is saying in this parable. It's important to know that Jesus is speaking to religious leaders in Jerusalem who are questioning Jesus' authority. Jesus is comparing the son who said he would work, but didn't, to these leaders. They only *appear* to be righteous but have, in fact, rejected Jesus. The son in the parable who actually did the work represents sinners. These are the people, who in spite of their initial disobedience to the Law, repent and find "the way of righteousness."

a) How does this remind you of Julian and Oliver in the first chapter of this book?

b) Can you think of a time when you said you would do something, but didn't?

c) Do both your words and actions serve God? How can you make sure you are not guilty of proclaiming to be a Christian, but not actually serving God?

Master and Servant ~ depicted in Chapter 1
Luke 17:7-10 (ESV)

"Will any one of you who has a servant plowing or keeping sheep say to him when he has come in from the field, 'Come at once and recline at table'? Will he not rather say to him, 'Prepare supper for me, and dress properly, and serve me while I eat and drink, and afterward you will eat and drink'? Does he thank

the servant because he did what was commanded? So you also, when you have done all that you were commanded, say, 'We are unworthy servants; we have only done what was our duty.'"

What do you do at home to help out your family? Do you have chores, like mowing the lawn, washing dishes, or doing laundry? Chances are you have some responsibility. It's nice when we are rewarded for doing something, isn't it? But does doing something you are supposed to do deserve a reward? In this parable, Jesus explains that our relationship with God is based on grace rather than works. The apostles have asked Jesus for more faith, and Jesus suggests they should not expect reward or praise for their service. Doing what God asks of us doesn't put God in our debt—it doesn't earn us a spot in His Kingdom. *Our salvation is a gift.* This parable may be difficult to read, as it seems as if Jesus approves of slavery. But he does not. It simply uses a situation common in Jesus' day to illustrate a spiritual truth.

a) Is Julian right to be upset in the first chapter of this book because his father doesn't praise him more for his work in the deli? Does Julian deserve a reward, in addition to his paycheck?

b) Do you feel you deserve praise or acknowledgment for serving God?

Lowest Seat at a Feast ~ depicted in Chapter 8
Luke 14:7-14 (ESV)

Now he told a parable to those who were invited, when he noticed how they chose the places of honor, saying to them, "When you are invited by someone to a wedding feast, do not sit down in a place of honor, lest someone more distinguished than you be invited by him, and he who invited you both will come and say to you, 'Give your place to this person,' and then you will begin with shame to take the lowest place. But when you are invited, go and sit in the lowest place, so that when your host comes he may say to you, 'Friend, move up higher.' Then you will be honored in the presence of all who sit at table with you. For everyone who exalts himself will be humbled, and he who humbles himself will be exalted."

He said also to the man who had invited him, "When you give a dinner or a banquet, do not invite your friends or your brothers or your relatives or rich neighbors, lest they also invite you in return and you be repaid. But when you give a feast, invite the poor, the crippled, the lame, the blind, and you will be blessed, because they cannot repay you. For you will be repaid at the resurrection of the just."

Have you ever bragged to a group of friends about something, like maybe a really cool vacation you had, or maybe an awesome test grade you earned? Imagine boasting to your friends, only to have another friend tell the group about her *even better* vacation, or his *even higher* test grade. That could feel a little embarrassing, right? The point Jesus is trying to make in the first part of the parable is that honor is awarded by God, and God honors the humble.

a) In Chapter 8 of this novel, who do you think represents the person taking "the seat of honor"?

b) Has someone ever boasted to you about something? How did it make you feel?

c) How can you be humble when you talk to God?

The Lost Sheep ~ depicted in Chapter 14
Matthew 18:12-14 (ESV)

"What do you think? If a man has a hundred sheep, and one of them has gone astray, does he not leave the ninety-nine on the mountains and go in search of the one that went astray? And if he finds it, truly, I say to you, he rejoices over it more than over the ninety-nine that never went astray. So it is not the will of my Father who is in heaven that one of these little ones should perish."

Do you have a favorite possession? Maybe it is your phone, a book, or a piece of jewelry that is special to you? What would you do if you lost this object? How much time would you spend looking for it? Chances are, if it were special to you, you wouldn't give up until you found it. It wouldn't matter if you had lots of other objects, would it? Nothing can replace what we hold dear. In this parable, Jesus explains that we, as Christians, are his sheep. The lost sheep represents a child of God who has sinned. But God holds us so dear that He would never stop looking for us.

a) In Chapter 14, how do Darla and Ollie react differently to the lost mouse?

b) How can people get lost, spiritually?

c) Have you ever experienced a time when you felt God was calling you back to Him?

Wise and Foolish Builders ~ depicted in Chapter 15
Luke 6:46-49 (ESV)

"Why do you call me 'Lord, Lord,' and not do what I tell you? Everyone who comes to me and hears my words and does them, I will show you what he is like: he is like a man building a house, who dug deep and laid the foundation on the rock. And when a flood arose, the stream broke against that house and could not shake it, because it had been well built. But the one who hears and does not do them is like a man who built a house on the ground without a foundation. When the stream broke against it, immediately it fell, and the ruin of that house was great."

Have you ever built a tower out of blocks? You don't have to be an architect to know that you need a solid base, a foundation, to keep the tower from tipping over. In this parable, Jesus explains to his disciples that they need a solid foundation as well. Did you figure out what that foundation is? If you said "Jesus," you are correct! Those who follow Jesus' teachings stand on solid ground.

a) How did Darla put into practice Jesus' words in Chapter 15?

b) How do you think Darla's "foundation" contributed to her choices?

c) Are there rules you know you should follow, but have a hard time doing so? How can you rely on God to help you with this?

Friend in Need ~ depicted in Chapter 18
Luke 11:5-8 (ESV)

And he said to them, "Which of you who has a friend will go to him at midnight and say to him, 'Friend, lend me three loaves, for a friend of mine has arrived on a journey, and I have nothing to set before him'; and he will answer from within, 'Do not bother me; the door is now shut, and my children are with me in bed. I cannot get up and give you anything'? I tell you, though he will not get up and give him anything because he is his friend, yet because of his impudence he will rise and give him whatever he needs."

Does prayer work? Well, that entirely depends on what you think the purpose of prayer is. If you think praying to God is equivalent to rubbing a magic lamp and getting wishes granted, then you are out of luck. When we pray continually, we experience the goodness of God. We become eager to do His will. And, of course, He blesses us with His fellowship and love. In this parable, Jesus is teaching His disciples about prayer. When someone, like the friend knocking on the door at midnight, refuses to go away, we are likely to give in to his requests. This is what Jesus says our attitude should be toward prayer—a persistent pursuit.

If we are persistent in asking for God to work in our lives, He will answer our prayers according to His perfect will and timing.

a) How is Darla, in Chapter 18, like the friend in the parable?

b) Can you think of a time you consistently prayed for something? What was the result?

c) How do you think your life could change if you started praying more regularly?

Unmerciful Servant ~ depicted in Chapter 23
Matthew 18:23-34 (ESV)

"Therefore the kingdom of heaven may be compared to a king who wished to settle accounts with his servants. When he began to settle, one was brought to him who owed him ten thousand talents. And since he could not pay, his master ordered him to be sold, with his wife and children and all that he had, and payment to be made. So the servant fell on his knees, imploring him, 'Have patience with me, and I will pay you everything.' And out of pity for him, the master of that servant released him and forgave him the debt. But when that same servant went out, he found one of his fellow servants who owed him a hundred denarii, and seizing him, he began to choke him, saying, 'Pay what you owe.' So his fellow servant fell down and pleaded with him, 'Have patience with me, and I will pay you.' He refused and went and put him in prison until he should pay the debt. When his fellow servants saw what had taken place, they were greatly distressed, and they

went and reported to their master all that had taken place. Then his master summoned him and said to him, 'You wicked servant! I forgave you all that debt because you pleaded with me. And should not you have had mercy on your fellow servant, as I had mercy on you?' And in anger his master delivered him to the jailers, until he should pay all his debt."

Have you ever yelled at someone? Lied? Broken something that didn't belong to you? There are millions of examples of how we can wrong people, and we are all guilty of many of them. Now think about a time when you apologized for hurting someone. It can be scary to admit you did something wrong. Did the person forgive you? If so, you can probably relate to this story. In this parable, Jesus is explaining how we receive forgiveness from God, and in return, God expects us to forgive one another.

a) In Chapter 23, we learn that Julian receives some form of forgiveness from his dad, aunt, and principal. How does he react to this?

b) Have you ever not forgiven someone for something? Do you feel this decision has helped you walk with Christ?

c) How can you work on forgiving others, even when it feels impossible?

"For it will be like a man going on a journey, who called his servants and entrusted to them his property. To one he gave five talents, to another two, to another one, to each according to his ability. Then he went away. He who had received the five talents went at once and traded with them, and he made five talents more. So also he who had the two talents made two talents more. But he who had received the one talent went and dug in the ground and hid his master's money. Now after a long time the master of those servants came and settled accounts with them. And he who had received the five talents came forward, bringing five talents more, saying, 'Master, you delivered to me five talents; here, I have made five talents more.' His master said to him, 'Well done, good and faithful servant. You have been faithful over a little; I will set you over much. Enter into the joy of your master.' And he also who had the two talents came forward, saying, 'Master, you delivered to me two talents; here, I have made two talents more.' His master said to him, 'Well done, good and faithful servant. You have been faithful over a little; I will set you over much. Enter into the joy of your master.' He also who had received the one talent came forward, saying, 'Master, I knew you to be a hard man, reaping where you did not sow, and gathering where you scattered no seed, so I was afraid, and I went and hid your talent in the ground. Here, you have what is yours.' But his master answered him, 'You wicked and slothful servant! You knew that I reap where I have not sown and gather where I scattered no seed? Then you ought to have invested my money with the bankers, and at my coming I should

have received what was my own with interest. So take the talent from him and give it to him who has the ten talents. For to everyone who has will more be given, and he will have an abundance. But from the one who has not, even what he has will be taken away. And cast the worthless servant into the outer darkness. In that place there will be weeping and gnashing of teeth.'"

Have you ever received a gift you didn't like? Maybe you put it up on a shelf, or in a closet, and forgot about it? How do you think the person who gave you that gift would feel if he knew you didn't use it? Probably not too good. This parable is about God's gifts to us, and He doesn't want us to stash those gifts on a shelf somewhere! God has given each of us gifts (maybe a certain skill, ability, or experience), and he wants us to use these gifts to glorify His kingdom. Just as each of the three servants receives different amounts of gold, not all gifts are the same. But the point of this parable is not how much or how little you get; it's what you do with what you have.

a) In Chapter 27, what talent does Ollie use to serve others? What might have happened if he hadn't helped?

b) What talents or skills do you have? How can you use them to serve God?

c) When thinking about your gifts from God, consider not only your talents but also things you enjoy doing. Could your interests or hobbies possibly be used to serve others? How?

The Rich Fool ~ depicted in Chapter 29
Luke 12:15-21 (ESV)

And he said to them, "Take care, and be on your guard against all covetousness, for one's life does not consist in the abundance of his possessions." And he told them a parable, saying, "The land of a rich man produced plentifully, and he thought to himself, 'What shall I do, for I have nowhere to store my crops?' And he said, 'I will do this: I will tear down my barns and build larger ones, and there I will store all my grain and my goods. And I will say to my soul, "Soul, you have ample goods laid up for many years; relax, eat, drink, be merry."' But God said to him, 'Fool! This night your soul is required of you, and the things you have prepared, whose will they be?' So is the one who lays up treasure for himself and is not rich toward God."

What do you do when you get too much Halloween candy? *Is* there such a thing as too much candy? If you think the answer is "No," then you might relate to the rich man in this story. He had so many crops that he built a second barn to store them. If you had two bags of candy, would you consider giving some away, or store some for later? If you chose to give some away, you are on the right track to following Jesus! In this parable, instead of using his crops to further the will of God, the rich man is only interested in accumulating his own wealth. Our lives are not about gathering wealth. Life is so much more than having an abundance of possessions.

a) How is Charlotte like the rich man in this parable?

b) Is there something in your life you don't like to share? Do you think you would feel better or worse if you chose to share?

c) What is something you can choose to share with others right now?

The Mustard Seed ~ depicted in Chapter 29
Mark 4:30-32 (ESV)

And he said, "With what can we compare the kingdom of God, or what parable shall we use for it? It is like a grain of mustard seed, which, when sown on the ground, is the smallest of all the seeds on earth, yet when it is sown it grows up and becomes larger than all the garden plants and puts out large branches, so that the birds of the air can make nests in its shade."

Have you ever given a stranger a compliment? Sent a thank-you note to a teacher? Offered help to a friend in need? These small acts of kindness have big, lasting effects on people. In this parable, Jesus is telling his disciples that the Kingdom of Heaven will develop from the smallest of beginnings into something that will be greater than anyone could have imagined. Think of the mustard seed as the Word of God. Christianity has successfully grown in the hearts of millions, yet it had humble beginnings. Christ doesn't enter as a mighty warrior, but as a lowly infant. He doesn't choose the most prestigious men to be his disciples; instead, he chooses ordinary people. So how are we like the mustard seed? Is it possible that every ordinary person is capable of great things? If you said "Yes," then this parable may be speaking directly to you!

a) How is Ollie's idea to photograph the shelter animals like a mustard seed?

b) What is something you can do that is perhaps insignificant, but can help others?

c) How will doing something to serve others help you to feel closer to God?

Workers in the Vineyard ~ depicted in Chapter 32
Matthew 20:1-16 (ESV)

"For the kingdom of heaven is like a master of a house who went out early in the morning to hire laborers for his vineyard. After agreeing with the laborers for a denarius a day, he sent them into his vineyard. And going out about the third hour he saw others standing idle in the marketplace, and to them he said, 'You go into the vineyard too, and whatever is right I will give you.' So they went. Going out again about the sixth hour and the ninth hour, he did the same. And about the eleventh hour he went out and found others standing. And he said to them, 'Why do you stand here idle all day?' They said to him, 'Because no one has hired us.' He said to them, 'You go into the vineyard too.' And when evening came, the owner of the vineyard said to his foreman, 'Call the laborers and pay them their wages, beginning with the last, up to the first.' And when those hired about the eleventh hour came, each of them received a denarius. Now when

those hired first came, they thought they would receive more, but each of them also received a denarius. And on receiving it they grumbled at the master of the house, saying, 'These last worked only one hour, and you have made them equal to us who have borne the burden of the day and the scorching heat.' But he replied to one of them, 'Friend, I am doing you no wrong. Did you not agree with me for a denarius? Take what belongs to you and go. I choose to give to this last worker as I give to you. Am I not allowed to do what I choose with what belongs to me? Or do you begrudge my generosity?' So the last will be first, and the first last."

Have you ever had a group project at school, where one member of the group doesn't do his or her fair share yet you all get the same grade, no matter how much each member contributed (or failed to contribute)? How did this make you feel? If you are like the workers in the story who started early in the morning, you might be angry. Why should they get the same amount of money as the others who worked less than half of the time than the early crew worked? In today's society, they would have a legitimate complaint—but the Kingdom of Heaven has a different sense of what's "fair" and what's not. Jesus is reminding the disciples that God's grace—our salvation—is a gift. Doesn't God have the right to give us a gift if He chooses? It is not given based on good deeds or merit, but at God's own discretion.

a) How does Ollie react when Julian receives a large gift from his father in Chapter 31?

b) Have you ever given someone a gift just because you wanted to? Could doing this help you feel closer to God? How?

c) Does knowing salvation is a gift affect how (or how often) you serve God? Why or why not?

The Prodigal Son ~ depicted in Chapter 32
Luke 15:11-32 (ESV)

And he said, "There was a man who had two sons. And the younger of them said to his father, 'Father, give me the share of property that is coming to me.' And he divided his property between them. Not many days later, the younger son gathered all he had and took a journey into a far country, and there he squandered his property in reckless living. And when he had spent everything, a severe famine arose in that country, and he began to be in need. So he went and hired himself out to one of the citizens of that country, who sent him into his fields to feed pigs. And he was longing to be fed with the pods that the pigs ate, and no one gave him anything.

"But when he came to himself, he said, 'How many of my father's hired servants have more than enough bread, but I perish here with hunger! I will arise and go to my father, and I will say to him, Father, I have sinned against heaven and before you. I am no longer worthy to be called your son. Treat me as one of your hired servants.' And he arose and came to his father. But while he was still a long way off, his father saw him and felt compassion, and ran and embraced him and kissed him. And the son said to him, 'Father, I have sinned against heaven and before you. I am no longer worthy to be called your son.' But the father said to his servants, 'Bring quickly the

best robe, and put it on him, and put a ring on his hand, and shoes on his feet. And bring the fattened calf and kill it, and let us eat and celebrate. For this my son was dead, and is alive again; he was lost, and is found.' And they began to celebrate.

"Now his older son was in the field, and as he came and drew near to the house, he heard music and dancing. And he called one of the servants and asked what these things meant. And he said to him, 'Your brother has come, and your father has killed the fattened calf, because he has received him back safe and sound.' But he was angry and refused to go in. His father came out and entreated him, but he answered his father, 'Look, these many years I have served you, and I never disobeyed your command, yet you never gave me a young goat, that I might celebrate with my friends. But when this son of yours came, who has devoured your property with prostitutes, you killed the fattened calf for him!' And he said to him, 'Son, you are always with me, and all that is mine is yours. It was fitting to celebrate and be glad, for this your brother was dead, and is alive; he was lost, and is found.'"

Have you ever sinned? If you answered, "No," that is probably a sin right there! We have all transgressed at some point in our lives, whether it is telling a lie, stealing, disobeying our parents, gossiping, or countless other offenses. Jesus is using this parable to teach many lessons, one of which is about forgiveness. The younger son has committed some obvious sins, but he returns home seeking repentance. Just as his father forgives him, our Heavenly Father will forgive us of our sins. But this parable also focuses on the older son, who is guilty of sin as well. When his younger brother returns, the older son is consumed by his resentment. He fails to understand his father's joy. The lesson Jesus is trying to teach is that no one is entitled to God's love and grace. It is a gift.

a) How are Julian and Ollie like the sons in this parable?

b) Do you ever need forgiveness from your parents? How would you feel if they didn't forgive you? How do you feel knowing that this is not an option with God—He will always forgive you?

c.) How does wanting others to receive God's love and forgiveness strengthen your relationship with Him?

About the Author

Bree Fortney has always enjoyed writing, working as a journalist, English instructor, and even an advice columnist, for more than twenty years. She earned a BA in English from Lynchburg University and an MA in English Literature from Longwood University. *Enlighten Me* is her debut Christian work.

To the detriment of her housework, Bree takes Genesis 2:2-3 very seriously, and enjoys an overabundance of hobbies, including reading, photography, painting, and above all, spending time with her family.